THE PRINCE AND THE PUCK

WILCOX WOMBATS
BOOK 4

DELANCEY STEWART

CHAPTER 1
DECK GILLESPIE
HOCKEY PLAYERS DO NOT DANCE

"QUIET DOWN, YOU JACKWADS," Coach Merritt said, looking down the line at the Wombats sitting along the bench, bent over with hands on knees, huffing and puffing, and standing expectantly against the boards. "Those LA turds aren't going to take it easy on you Tuesday, and I sure as hell haven't this week either. You guys deserve your day off and it's been a long week, so I won't keep you too long, but we need to talk about one thing."

"Wasn't too bad, always worth it when we get to see Corny yak," Rock Stevens called out, earning dirty looks from both the coach and from Tyler "Corny" Cornwall, who was finally getting some color back in his face.

"Look, I need to give you a guys a heads up is all," Coach went on.

I exchanged a look with John Samuels, our starting goalie. Last time we got a 'heads up,' we found out Mizzoni was leaving and Samuels was becoming the youngest starting goalie the FHL had ever seen. It turned out to be a good move. Maybe this news would work out well too. I hoped so—this team was more than just my job. It was my family and my foreseeable future.

"You ever heard of the Savannah Bananas?" Coach went on.

"Like…the dancing baseball guys?" Sly Remington asked.

"Exactly," Coach said. "Had you ever heard of them before they were the dancing baseball guys?"

I did not like where this was heading one bit. I couldn't dance to save my life. If that was going to be a new prerequisite for being on the team, I was in trouble.

"Sir," Cade Simpson interjected, his deep baritone coming from somewhere within his massive red beard. "Are we going to have to dance while we play hockey?"

Coach scrubbed a hand down his jaw. "Lord, I hope not," he said. "Listen, first of all, this was not my idea. Second, you're all going to be good sports and comply."

"He's totally making us dance," Solamentes said. "But it's okay. I got moooves." He gyrated his hips as he said this and for a second I thought Corny might not be the only one to lose his lunch today.

"No dancing!" Coach roared.

We immediately shut up, all the little side conversations cut off abruptly. No one wanted to be sent back out to do Herbies until we did puke.

"The thing is, I guess the owner thinks we have a publicity problem," Coach continued. "And he's brought in some kind of consultant to help us fix it."

"PR problem?" Samuels asked, voicing what we were all thinking. "What does that mean?"

The coach looked up to the ceiling and then let his gaze slide around the empty stands in the arena. "Honestly? I have no clue. But I don't ask questions that might put my job at risk and I suggest you yahoos don't either. This PR guy is coming in to help bolster the image of the Wilcox Wombats, and you're going to cooperate, whether that means dancing on the ice or signing more autographs or kissing babies, or whatever."

"Kissing babies?" Panther Aspen mouthed, looking bewildered.

"The rep will be here tomorrow morning to do some initial interviews," Coach finished. "Be nice."

With that, the coach turned and headed back to his office, leaving us to exchange confused looks and get ourselves cleaned up to go home.

We'd be facing the Cruisers on Tuesday, and tomorrow would be the only day off we'd get this week. That meant tonight was my favorite night of the week, the only night when I could really relax—stay up late, play video games, and maybe even sneak one little drink in.

I was just about to pour a couple fingers of Scotch when my phone rang. One look at the screen and I decided to pour myself a whole hand instead of just two fingers. I capped the Scotch and took a healthy sip before answering.

"Hey, Dad. Mom."

"Son." My parents had never been big on affectionate greetings. This was their version of gushing.

"How are things?" I asked, sinking into the dark brown leather couch that faced the big screen on which I'd be playing video games later. For now, I had a tape of our last game going with the volume off.

"Much the same, Declan," Dad said. Mom was a bit more conversational, though.

"We miss you, honey."

"I miss you guys too," I said, though it was hard to decide whether that was really true. I hadn't seen my parents in person in almost five years. I missed the idea of them, but I wasn't sure if I really missed them. "How's Lamb?"

My mother released a frazzled sigh at that. "He is… Lambert. About the same. Adequate, I guess?"

"Barely," Dad added.

My older brother had been a bit of a handful since he hit puberty, and neither age nor maturity had seemed to do much to calm him down. I would have said it was pretty much impossible to get into too much trouble back home— the place was restrictive, to say the least—but Lambert always seemed to manage.

"I'm sure he'll straighten out soon," I said, but even I wasn't certain. I hadn't talked to my brother since the last time I was home, when he made it pretty clear that his acting out was all my fault. I left him wearing the mantel of responsibility. Literally. I didn't like the distance between us, but he'd rebuffed every effort I'd made to reach out. And lately, I hadn't made many.

"We have watched your latest games," my father said. "I don't feel like you are playing enough to warrant—"

"Dad." I didn't want to hear this again.

"I just wish you were here, Son."

"This was decided years ago. You let me go."

"We didn't know it would be forever," Mom said.

"It's not," I told her, exasperated with the same conversation we always seemed to have. "But I'll play as long as I can. And then I'll figure out what's next."

Dad coughed then, unleashing a horrendous gravelly cacophony over the line, and Mom's concerned voice said, "Erik. Dear…" There was some muffled sound then, and Mom came back on.

"Maybe we'll see you soon," she said, sounding tired.

"Maybe," I said, knowing it was extremely unlikely. I didn't have time in the season to travel that far. And my parents were certainly not coming to see me.

"Be well Deckkie. We love you." Mom didn't wait for me to respond before ending the call.

And that was why I didn't love chatting with my family. There were certain…extenuating circumstances surrounding my life that I preferred not to dwell upon, and talking to Mom and Dad brought them all back. I couldn't help but feel like I was shirking some kind of responsibility to them, staying away. But they'd agreed to this when I was ten, allowing me to move to the United States to live with my Uncle Jericho in Colorado. They allowed me to follow my dreams, away from the restrictions of the life I was born to.

And as far as I was concerned, there were no take-backsies.

I took another sip of the Scotch, scowling at the glass and thinking better of the enormous pour I'd given myself. Once I'd swapped it for a cup of tea instead, I settled myself again and started my game, doing my best to put any thoughts of whatever was or was not happening at home out of my mind.

CHAPTER 2
LIZZY CANFIELD

PR AND ESPIONAGE. SAME THING.

I WAS EXHAUSTED. A twelve-hour plane ride was not my idea of a good time. Add to that the fact the town of Wilcox was not exactly a major hub, and that meant another lengthy car ride. At least that had been arranged ahead of time. All I'd had to do was get off the plane and everything else was handled.

There were a few perks to my job.

The enormous flat that had been rented and furnished on my behalf was one of them.

"You're sure this is mine?" I asked the doorman who'd helped me up to the eighth floor with my suitcases and handed me the key.

"Absolutely," he said, giving me a knowing and somewhat fatherly smile. "I hope you'll be comfortable here. I've been instructed to ensure you have everything you could possibly need."

I turned and gaze around at the immense open floorpan, the floor-to-ceiling windows, and the modern furnishings.

My place back home was a far cry from all this, namely that my place back home was one I shared with my mother. "I think I'll be just fine here, uh…?"

"Arnold," the man said, smiling again.

"I'm Lizzy."

He nodded. He knew that already. Of course.

"You need anything, Miss Lizzy, and I'm right downstairs."

I offered him a smile that I knew looked tired, but I hoped felt genuine. "Thank you."

He backed out, nodding and bowing a little bit as he pulled the door to the flat shut. I moved quickly and bolted it. Then, I did a quick perimeter walk, and finally scouted for bugs.

There was no real reason there would be any devices, but old habits died hard. And technically, I was on an assignment. It just looked a whole lot different from most of my regular assignments.

Everything suddenly looked a whole lot different.

I stood in front of those enormous windows, gazing down on the town of Wilcox and wondering about the man I'd been sent here to find. I hadn't seen him in person in years. And the last time we'd seen one another, he probably hadn't noticed me. That was the nature of our positions, of course.

It'd been different when we were kids. Funny how rules of propriety seemed to be unnecessary when you were little. We probably should have known better, but we did what we did anyway. It was my mother who probably would have faced consequences, had there been any—for allowing her daughter to step outside the clear confines drawn by her position. But there never were any.

And so Declan and I had been friends.

We'd played hide and seek—lord knew at his house there were plenty of places to hide. We'd played video games and watched movies and sports together. And since we were the same age, we'd even been taught together by the in-home educators his parents paid for.

And when we were little, I'd given it very little thought.

Just like I'd given little thought to the fact that Declan was my first crush, the first boy to hold my hand, and the first boy to ever kiss me—if you could count a tiny peck at nine years old that was followed by hysterical giggles on both our parts.

We'd been young, and neither of us had been bogged down by responsibility.

But now?

Everything had changed.

CHAPTER 3
DECK

THIS STOOL IS IN MY BUSINESS

MONDAY MORNING I headed into practice and was immediately cornered by Coach Merritt. "Get suited up and then head into the office next to mine," he said, his tone every bit as friendly as ever—meaning not at all friendly.

"Uh, okay…" I wanted to ask why, but I didn't want to get my head bit off.

"The PR consultant is in there."

"Oh."

Great.

I headed for the locker room and then did as I was told, stepping into the small office, which was mostly dark. There was someone in there, but she was hard to see since a huge ring light stood between me and her.

"Hey, hi," I said. "Coach told me to come in and… uh… help?"

"Oh, hi, yes." There was a clatter as the woman I couldn't quite see dropped something to the floor and leaned down to pick it up.

"Do you need help?"

"No, no," she sounded flustered, and I felt a little sorry for her. "I've got it. Just have a seat there, okay?"

"Sure." I looked at the stool set in front of the glaring light. There was a microphone on top of it, one of those tiny ones people pinned to their shirts. "The mic?"

"Oh yeah, you're going to talk into that while I record," she said, not looking at me. She was gathering papers together onto the clipboard she'd dropped.

"So I just… hold this microphone here?" I asked, perching on the stool that felt about thirteen sizes too small squeezed between my butt cheeks. Shouldn't they have sized this interview setup for hockey players? Seeing as how they were going to be interviewing… hockey players?

"Yep, perfect. Just like that." The new team PR consultant nodded from where she stood on the other side of the ring light currently blazing in my eyes.

The stool felt a bit as if it was becoming a part of me, a new appendage attached in a place I most definitely didn't need to be introducing a new item.

"Hey, uh, would it be okay if I stood? This stool is a bit invasive."

"The stool?" The woman asked. "Invasive?"

"Yeah, my butt… listen, never mind. I'm gonna stand, okay?" I pushed the stool back and stood, holding the microphone awkwardly. "Okay. Perfect. Are you going to ask me questions?"

"Uh, right. Questions. Okay." The new PR consultant the team had brought in did not—in my humble opinion—appear to know a good goddamned thing about PR. Not that I was an expert, but this lady hadn't even introduced herself yet. She looked like a deer in headlights (a very fit deer in headlights—seriously, even with the bright light in my eyes I could see she had guns some of the guys on the team would envy. I wanted to ask her about her protein supplementation strategy, but that would have to wait.)

"What's your name again?" I asked her now.

"Lizzy Canfield."

"Okay, Lizzy. Well, I've got practice in a minute and kinda need to get going, so let's do the questions, okay?"

She nodded, shuffling through a bunch of note cards in her hands.

"So you're—"

"Deck Gillespie. Left wing for the Wombats."

"Right. And this is your—"

"Third season."

"Tell me about your childhood, Deck. Did you always know you wanted to play pro hockey?"

That was actually a funny question, but I couldn't tell her that.

In my country, hockey wasn't a sport you could play, thanks to the sweltering heat and general lack of square footage. No, hockey was pretty much the dividing line between my former life and my current one. The line had been drawn when I was only ten and I was pretty intent on keeping it firmly in place.

"Yep, pretty much from the beginning. I was playing for a travel team here in Virginia when I was twelve."

"And… you're from Colorado originally? Or Virginia? My notes aren't clear."

"Colorado is close enough." Ha, not even close. Another question I couldn't answer truthfully.

"So your family is supportive of your career?"

"Doesn't really matter, does it? I'm here now."

Lizzy's eyebrows went up and a strange look crossed her pretty face.

She was pretty, I noticed, now that my eyes had adjusted a little bit and she'd stepped closer to the camera aimed at me. Long dark hair pulled back into a low ponytail. Pouty dark-painted lips, and wide dark eyes. And then there was the body. I'd always been partial to women who looked like they could potentially kick my ass. It created a fun dynamic in other wrestling-type activities. Not that Lizzy and I would be partaking in any of those together.

Also, Lizzy was basically a coworker, and the team had a strict no fraternization rule. Plus, she was a distraction. In my opinion, this whole PR thing was a distraction, but I was not going to argue.

"So what do you bring to the Wombats?" she asked me now.

"Power, speed. Good looks. Charisma," I laughed.

"And your intention is to stay on the team for the foreseeable future?"

"Um. Yes. Wait, why? Did you hear something?" That question made me nervous. Was I being cut? Traded? Had Dad finally succeeded at working some kind of deal to get me fired?

"No, of course not. Just trying to drive at your commitment."

"I'm committed," I assured her, maybe a little too vehemently. I checked my watch, realizing I was going to be late for practice if we didn't wrap this up. And being late was not how I wanted to demonstrate my commitment. "Lizzy? I'm gonna have to catch you later. Practice and all."

"Of course. Thanks, Declan."

I handed Lizzy the microphone back, and was halfway out of the room when I realized she'd used my full name. Which I definitely had not told her. Of course, it was probably on the official roster, but everyone in the states called me Deck.

Weird.

And those questions… If these were the kinds of things the public relations effort was going to focus on, it was not going to make us a household name. Maybe the subject of some biting jokes or recommended nap time fodder for infants…

"Deck! You're late!" Coach hollered.

"Your PR lady," I explained, pointing a thumb behind me as I hustled toward the locker room.

The coach rolled his eyes. "Don't remind me."

I laced my skates and stepped out onto the ice with the rest of the Wombats for practice. I just needed to keep my nose clean, my history hidden, and my record impressive. Pretty little PR ladies with pouty lips were definitely not my concern.

CHAPTER 4
LIZZY

DON'T BE SARCASTIC WITH THE
KING...

"YOUR MAJESTY, forgive me saying, but this is a little bit ridiculous." I realized I was hissing, but I couldn't really have a private call in the confines of the Wombats Arena. For the majority of those who might overhear, the conversation would certainly be confusing. For one player in particular, it would set off more red flags and alarms than the historic invasion of our home country by the Durnish forces back in the sixties.

"Eliza, I know it's a lot to ask, but your particular skill set would suggest your ability to convince my son of his true place and convince him that it is time for him to come home. As soon as possible." The Queen still spoke to me like the child who used to play with her son.

"It would be easier if I were allowed to jump him from behind and take him down with a sleeper hold first," I said, "then I would have a better chance of accomplishing the goal."

"Do not injure the prince," the king said sternly. He did

not sound ill, though his cancer diagnosis had been the event that prompted my own presence here. With the king ill and the heir looking somewhat unreliable, the spare heir was needed. As soon as possible.

"Of course not, I won't hurt him." I hated being on speaker at the palace. The king and queen tended to take my calls together, and it was somewhat overwhelming having all that royal direction at one time.

"This is a very delicate situation," the king reminded me. "Declan needs to come back of his own free will. He cannot be coerced. And no one there can know his true identity until he has accepted his position here at home—it would put him in grave danger."

"Of course, sir."

"So what is the problem? We have arranged the perfect entry for you," the Queen said, sounding slightly annoyed.

"The biggest issue is that I don't know anything about PR. This entire set up is so far-fetched, I have no idea how I'll keep up the charade in any kind of convincing way."

"The team's owner accepted it," the king reminded me. Of course, there'd been a sizable donation to make it happen.

"Right, but what will the coach think when I spend hours lurking around doing 'PR' things and nothing really comes from it except maybe the loss of one of his most valuable players?"

"He will accept that the sovereign prince of Murdan was urgently required to return to his born duty. He will accept that an American hockey coach does not stand in the way of royal destiny." King Erik had a way of phrasing things that made them sound already decided.

"Right. Sure."

"Are you using sarcasm with your king?" The Queen asked.

"Just a tiny bit. Sorry."

The king sighed. "I know this is a complex task, Lizzy. That's why we chose you. Your record of service is outstanding, and your loyalty to our nation is unparalleled. If anyone can convince my son to realize that his real purpose is at home, and that he has little choice in the matter, I believe it is you."

"Sir, is there any chance we are potentially conflating my performance in special operations with the need for someone who can act and persuade? My persuasion techniques generally involve weapons or torture."

"Do not torture the prince." The Queen was definitely sounding annoyed now.

"Of course not, I'm just suggesting—"

"You are the person for the job. Convince him." King Erik directed.

"Of course."

"Check in tomorrow," he said.

"Yes, Your Majesties." I shoved my phone into my pocket and rolled my eyes. This was not exactly the cherry position I'd hoped would be mine coming out of the commendations I'd received on the tail of my last assignment. If a low-paid acting job surrounded by men who considered playing a game to be a respectable profession was my due, maybe I should have allowed that terrorist dictator to stay where he was... But no, I didn't regret my past. Even though there was a good chance I was going to regret my future.

I deleted the interview I'd done with the prince. Not only did it not move me closer to my mission objective, it was useless in general. Somehow, I needed to put together a scintillating public relations campaign about this ice hockey team. Maybe I should start with why they'd been named after an animal that didn't even exist on the North American continent.

Ah yes, Lizzy. Your instincts for compelling entertainment will serve you well. Who doesn't want to learn more about wombats?

I was so screwed.

CHAPTER 5

DECK

LUXURY = A LONG SHOWER

THE PRACTICE ROOMS had mostly cleared out by the time I ended the world's longest hot shower. The trainers were clearing things up, and there wasn't another player around.

I liked the place this way. Quiet and empty. It made me feel like I could do anything I liked and no one would be bothered. Of course the only thing I generally did was take stupidly long showers. Not that I couldn't do that at home, but there was something about the locker room shower—the reality of being here, on this team, in this place.

It was what I'd always dreamed about. Once I knew what hockey was, of course. Before that, I'd simply dreamed of America. The space, the freedom. The anonymity.

It wasn't that my life at home was bad. Far from it. Most kids would probably say they'd kill to be awoken by three butlers carrying trays of food and picking up after them as they moved through their four-room apartment on the way to say hello to Mom and Dad. But those kids hadn't thought that dream through. They didn't know about the weight of responsibility that came with being the spare heir, about the expectations on everything from whether you used your finger bowl correctly to if you addressed the right duke in the right way in the right order when a bunch of frilly dudes showed up at court to chat up your dad. The king.

It felt like I'd been seeking an escape since the day I realized my position. I knew I didn't want it. I didn't want any of what my dad did all day—worrying about international relations, mitigating in-country battles between factions, and monitoring public sentiment around taxes and housing costs. No thanks.

I had spent my days bribing attendants to get me old DVDs of American sports matches. Baseball, football, and of course—ice hockey. It was all I wanted to think about, to learn about, to do.

Lucky for me, I was number two. Lambert was born first, like it or not, and so he didn't have the same kind of freedom I did. Did I ever feel bad for him? Sure, but there were probably benefits to being the future king. I just couldn't imagine what they might be. He could have them.

Mom and Dad were happy enough to let me go (taking my athletics obsession and constant begging for a palace hockey rink with me.) Dad had a distant cousin in Colorado, and while I'd never been there, the place sounded a lot like heaven to me. A private school with other boys? A suburban home with my own bedroom and no valets or butlers in sight? The chance to join sports teams? I was in.

I was sent to Colorado to meet Uncle Jericho, who wasn't my uncle at all.

That was when my life began.

I might not have been the most athletically inclined kid by genetics, but what I lacked in natural ability I made up for in sheer grit. I wanted it more than anyone else.

And after a lot of help from Uncle Jericho, lots and lots of practices and camps, and lots of years of working my ass off, I got it.

I sighed happily, gathering my bag to my shoulder and heading for the back door to let myself out into the player's lot.

"Night Deck," Al called.

"Have a good night, Al."

Al was the security guard who patrolled the arena overnight. He was a good guy, and I often thought about how if I couldn't play hockey, I might be happy to do a job like his, or maybe like Julius, who drove the ice cleaner. Just to be here. To be this free.

Though, the playing was a lot of fun too.

The parking lot was dim in the graying light, and my car sat almost alone beneath the lone lamp post. I grabbed my keys out of my pocket and froze, the hair on the back of my neck suddenly standing on end.

Spinning around, I realized I wasn't alone.

The PR lady. She was just coming around the corner of the building, strutting in a way that told me she didn't have a care in the world, despite wearing three-inch heels and a sheath dress that hugged her muscular curves.

She did have a care, though. She just didn't know it.

I spotted the two guys on the other side of the lot closing in on her fast. They wore dark cargoes and T-shirts, and moved like panthers gliding through the shadows.

I let my bag slide from my shoulder to the pavement and took a steady breath, readying myself.

The guys were closing in on us now, and if they thought they were going to assault this woman right here in front of me, they had another think coming.

"Lizzy!" I hissed, but she was already angling toward me, practically breaking into a run. I was surprised at her hustle, given the heels.

"Deck, get in your car, now!"

She was awfully bossy for a woman in danger, I thought. And oddly chivalrous.

I hit the unlock button so she could get in and lock the doors, but she actually detoured, coming to my side just as the two men broke into a dead sprint, heading right for us.

"Shit, what are you—?" But there was no time for questions.

I tried to throw myself in front of Lizzy, but she was actually doing the exact same thing, and her erratic behavior threw me off balance. Why wouldn't this woman let me just save her?

The two men reached her just as I went down, hard, on the pavement, but I shot a foot out and tripped one of the guys, landing him next to me. I just had to hope Lizzy could hold off the other guy for a minute while I dealt with this one.

Adrenaline surged through me when I saw that the attacker held a baton in one hand and had a knife sheathed at his belt. I rolled, moving to straddle him, but he slid out from beneath me, reversing our positions so fast I didn't see it coming. He got in a good strike with the baton that would have knocked me out if I hadn't blocked with my forearm. He was almost on top of me a second later, and I managed to buck up enough to keep him from pinning me.

There was a lot of grunting and groaning, but I got a solid blow in to the guy's nose just before he slid off me suddenly, clearly changing his mind about taking me on.

"Lizzy!" I yelled, getting to my feet.

The other guy had her from behind, and I bolted to rescue her, hoping this wasn't going to end badly.

CHAPTER 6
LIZZY

LETTING THE PRINCE DEFEND ME.
SORT OF.

I SHOULD HAVE BEEN PAYING MORE attention. But who the hell knew Declan would require an eight-hour shower after practice? I must've walked the perimeter forty times before the enormous prince finally emerged from the players' door, grinning around himself like there was nothing in the world to worry about.

Sigh. Royalty.

I was just going to stroll on by—the guy was so oblivious he didn't even see me—but that was when I saw the two men beelining for him across the parking lot.

If I pulled my sidearm, the jig would be up, so I'd already begun visualizing how I'd disable the men in hand to hand when Deck yelled out my name, giving me away.

"Dammit," I grumbled, throwing myself in front of him and knocking him out of the way as the first man reached us.

Within seconds, I'd disarmed goon number one,

throwing his knife across the lot as Declan tripped the second man. Good thinking.

It took me only a few seconds to counter the attacker, and I was another second away from knocking him unconscious, when the man Deck was scrabbling with got the upper hand and climbed onto the prince's chest.

Two on one was not my favorite fighting style, but it wouldn't be the first time. I threw my weight to the side, pulling man number one with me and then slammed a kick into the other guy's side, knocking him off the prince.

Unfortunately, that was when the first guy managed to slip behind me, trying to get me in a lock.

"Not today," I bit out, gathering my strength as I bucked forward, tossing him over my shoulder. That was going to hurt us both in the morning, but he seemed to realize he wasn't going to win this fight and he and his friend both scrambled away.

Shit. It seemed more critical than ever that I convince Declan to head home sooner rather than later.

The prince was at my side a second later, his big hands on my upper arms, his wide blue eyes peering down at me worriedly.

"Why didn't you get in the car?" he asked.

"Why didn't you get in the car?" I asked him back.

"And leave you to those thugs?"

Ohhh, right. I was the defenseless woman in this scenario. I kept forgetting that. Shit, I was a bad actress. The thing was, I didn't want to play scared and pathetic because I wasn't. Far from it. I shrugged. "I probably would have been okay."

"I'm just glad I was able to scare them both off," Declan said, causing me to gape at him, openmouthed. Did he actually believe he'd just won that fight on his own?

"Um. Yeah. Okay, we'll go with that."

"He didn't hurt you, did he?" Deck had moved on to examining me for injuries. "Should we call the police or report this to management?"

I sighed, brushing my dress straight and pushing the escaped strands of hair back into the low ponytail. I bent down to pick up the stilettos I'd ditched the second the fight had begun. "I think I'm fine," I said. "Just shaken up, I guess." That sounded good, right? Defenseless women were shaken up by fights.

"Anyone would be," he said. "I really feel like we ought to do something. Report this?"

I shook my head. The police were no match for anti-monarchist terrorists gunning for the likely heir. "I think we're okay, right?"

Declan nodded.

"I'll mention it to the rink security tomorrow, but it was probably just a random thing." I couldn't tell him the truth. Those guys had seemed like the B-team, though. I worried about who they'd send next time. "We're fine. We should probably just get home, lock our doors."

Deck chuckled lightly. "Maybe I'm a little shaken up too. Could I..." he raised a hand, rubbing it across his jaw in a surprisingly boyish gesture. "Would you maybe want to get a drink? Just calm the nerves a bit?"

If he was going out, I wasn't letting him out of my sight.

"Yeah, okay," I told him, smiling. "That's a good idea. Is

there somewhere nearby? Maybe a place with a couple entrances and good lighting?"

Declan's lips lifted on one side, and I realized—not for the first time—how handsome he had become. I wondered if he remembered me at all, but of course, the context was all wrong. I didn't look a thing like I had as a child, and I went by a different name too.

"Weirdly specific," he said. "But I like a girl who knows what she wants. I'll drive."

CHAPTER 7
DECK

PRINCE PINK WINE

LIZZY THE PR girl was oddly unruffled as we rode around the corner to the Teakhouse Tavern, one of the team's usual hangs when we were in town.

We stepped into the bar, which was quiet since it was a Monday evening. I dropped a hand to Lizzy's back out of habit—and partially because I wanted to touch her—but she sidestepped me and pointed to the back corner.

"Over there."

I looked to the remote booth where she was pointing. I liked to sit at the bar—a little see and be seen never hurt anyone. But there was no one in here to see or be seen by, so I agreed. Plus, I was pretty curious about Lizzy.

"I'll grab drinks and meet you over there?"

She nodded and then I watched her strut to the corner, making a survey of the entire bar visually before sliding into the far bench with her back to the wall.

She was quirky. I liked quirky, I decided. She also hadn't told me what she wanted to drink.

Not a problem though. Since joining the ranks of elite athletes in the United States, I'd gotten a pretty good sense of what the average American woman drank when out at a bar with me.

"A white zinfandel and Macallan, neat."

Lex, the bartender who'd been here since I started playing for the team, nodded and moved efficiently behind the bar, getting my drinks. I carried them over to the table and set them on the surface, and then slid into the booth across from Lizzy.

Before I could say a word, she'd picked up my Scotch and sipped. I waited for her to make a face and hand it back to me, laughing about how she didn't know how I could drink that stuff. But that isn't what happened.

Instead, she lifted an eyebrow, tilted her head toward the wine, and said, "I wouldn't have pegged you for a pink wine guy."

I shrugged. "Just trying something different, I guess." I sipped the wine, working hard not to be the one to make a face.

So Lizzy drank Scotch.

Interesting.

"So," I said, searching for something charming that might counter the idea she now had that I drank pink wine and didn't conclusively prevail in parking lot fights with assholes. "Did you grow up here in Virginia, Lizzy?"

"Ah, no," she said, sipping my Scotch again and appearing to savor it. She offered nothing else.

"So," I started again, "been in public relations long?"

"Not long."

"But you must be a killer when it comes to image or something. Or else they wouldn't have sent you to the Wombats, right?"

"A killer for sure," she said, and a smirk passed her lips. She stayed quiet another minute, enjoying my drink as I struggled through the wine, and finally I got a little desperate.

"Lizzy, I didn't really mean to force you to come hang out. I have the sense maybe you have other things to do?" It was rare to be the more interested party on a date—if that's what this was—but something about Lizzy's ambivalence made me feel slightly desperate. Not a good look.

"You needed a glass of pink wine. I didn't want to stand in the way of that."

"I could have come to drink pink wine alone," my voice sounded slightly biting, even to me.

She raised an eyebrow at me. Something in the expression gave me a flash of recognition. Lizzy reminded me of someone I used to know. A girl I played with when I was a kid, back in Murdan. My mom's assistant's daughter, Eliza. She sighed. "Yeah. I'm sorry. Maybe I'm more shook up than I thought."

I stared at her, sitting there, completely put together and calm. If this was a woman shook up, I had a lot more to learn about women.

CHAPTER 8
LIZZY

A PROPOSAL. BUT NOT AN
INDECENT ONE.

I KNEW I was fucking this up.

But my ego was struggling with allowing me to play the role I needed to play to accomplish my mission. The thing was, I was pretty sure I could simply subdue the prince and get him on the plane. Tonight. In the next ten minutes, probably.

However, my instructions were crystal clear.

I wasn't to use force, and I was not to let the prince know who I was or why I was really here. He had to come back to the crown of his own accord, or the potential for a reversed secession would not be valid and Lambert would retain his place in line. Something no one—I was guessing especially Lambert—wanted to see happen. But with the king's failing health and Lambert's situation, there was one clear choice for the next ruler of Murdan. Only, that person believed he'd given up any claims he had on the crown more than a decade ago and never looked back.

I needed to get myself in check. Quickly.

"Yeah, that was just pretty scary," I tried, aware that my face and body language were not saying "scared."

"It was," Declan agreed.

"And I mean… I'm just pretty new to the area, and to the job."

"How did you end up in the job?" he asked. "If you're not super experienced? Is that rude to ask?"

"No," I said, my mind scrabbling for a lie. "Fair question. My agency was going to send someone else, but he got called away on a last-minute opportunity to film rhinos in Africa."

"Rhinos won out over hockey?"

I laughed. "Believe it or not, yeah. So you get me."

"Well, I hope you won't take this the wrong way," he said. "But whatever it is you're doing better be amazing. And maybe no dancing."

"Dancing?"

"Like the Bananas, I mean."

I had no idea what the man was on about. Had the pink wine gone to his head so fast? I was going to ask another question, but he started talking again.

"It'd be great to be seen as the team to beat," he said. "And I wouldn't mind if it helped secure my place on the team too."

"You think your place isn't secure?" I asked.

"I'm not the player getting endorsement deals yet, no."

"That's important to you?"

"Let's just say I have reasons to want to be indispensable here."

I nodded, wishing he was slightly less dedicated to the team. It would make my job easier.

"Lizzy," Declan said, leaning in slightly and wrinkling his forehead. "I have a proposal for you."

A proposal? Unless it involved him suggesting that his whole life in the States had been a huge mistake and wondering if I might like to take a trip to tropical island destination right this minute and meet his family, I didn't think it was a proposal I was going to like.

"Umm."

"Don't say no."

"I can't say anything until I know what your proposal involves. Typically the word proposal comes with certain expectations."

He let out a laugh and then sat back in the booth. "Lizzy. We just met."

Not strictly true, but as far as he knew it was.

"Are you saying you'd like to marry me? Am I that devastatingly attractive?" He grinned, and I fought off the urge to tell him that he was.

Because the fact was, he definitely was.

He was made from stacks of hard, bulging muscle, skated like a demon or some Norse horseman bent on revenge, and had sapphire blue eyes I still saw in my dreams. He'd been ridiculously handsome when we were nine years old, and he'd only grown hotter with time.

Our history—which he clearly didn't recall—and my attraction to him were two of the main reasons I'd tried like hell to turn down this job.

"I do not want to marry you," I assured him, ignoring the little girl inside me who had wanted exactly that.

"Then let's talk about my idea," he said, finishing his wine. "But first, I think I might like to get a glass of what you've got. Another?"

I shook my head and waited while he went back to the bar, returning with a glass of single malt.

Shit. The only thing working against him—a taste for low quality wine—had just evaporated.

I watched his throat work as he sipped the Scotch and forced myself not to react. Damn, this was going to be harder than I thought.

CHAPTER 9
DECK

LAME-O MOVIES WITH SUBTITLES

LIZZY WAS CUTE.

No, that wasn't the right word, though the faint blush climbing her round cheeks was cute. Lizzy, as a total package, was smoking hot.

I'd heard a few of the guys discussing her in the locker room as I'd prepared for my shower, and I hadn't disagreed with their assessments one bit. Tight, curvy body with muscles that only served to emphasize her appeal. I wasn't a guy for skinny model types who looked like they might break if you touched them the wrong way. I wasn't looking for a woman at all, but if I had been, it'd be a woman like this one.

Built for action. Built for speed. Built for… all the things I would very much like to do with her in various places and positions.

Shit.

Down, boy.

I shifted my weight and continued with my proposal.

"Let me help you."

The eyebrow went up again. "Help me? What do you think I need help with?"

I was beginning to see that Lizzy was a very independent woman. She didn't even like the suggestion that she might need help. How, I wondered, had she ended up in a job she was clearly not cut out for?

"With the PR. Let's make a movie. Like a documentary, except good."

Lizzy stared at me. "You want to help me do my job?"

I nodded. "I've watched a lot of American television and movies."

She tilted her head and gave me a tiny smile as if she'd just caught me in a lie or something. "American? As opposed to…"

Shit. I hadn't meant to say that. "Yeah. American. Like me." I took a sip of my Scotch, which would be my last since we had a game the next day. "You know, regular stuff. Mainstream."

"Uh huh."

"Not lame-o foreign stuff with subtitles."

"Yeah, got it."

"So I think I'm prepared to help you make the Wombats documentary really awesome. We'll keep the pacing fast, and do a bunch of shots where we move quick between a player talking and then him doing his thing on the ice. Lots of pounding music and then some deeper storyline running through the whole thing. I wonder if any of the guys has a three-legged cat or something…"

"That would help how?"

"By making him really sympathetic. Maybe someone has a sick hamster or something. I'll ask around. What do you think?" I'd talked myself completely into it.

She shook her head. "I don't think a sick hamster is going to be the difference between this PR campaign being good and this campaign getting me fired." She made an adorable face as she said that, and I realized her job was probably really important to her. Or maybe she had an asshole boss. I tried to be more empathetic.

"Shit. I hadn't thought of that. You're really under pressure here." We were alike in that way.

"Kind of, yeah." She shrugged, tilting her head so her smooth dark ponytail slid over one shoulder. I forbid myself from considering what it would feel like to grip it in my hand while I guided her head to my—nope. Forbidden. Not thinking about that.

"Okay, so what ideas do you have?" I asked her.

"Well, I was going to interview everyone to start, and then go from there. Maybe kind of build on whoever has the best story. Maybe a coming up from nothing kinda thing."

"So you want Rubio for that. Grew up in East Los Angeles, super tough neighborhood. Ended up going to some camp put on by a former Wombats player."

She nodded and made a note in her phone. "Okay, good. Who else?"

I thought about my teammates.

"Elks might be a good one to chat with. His older brother played hockey too. He was always in the guy's shadow. Then his brother died in a car crash, so now he says he channels him while he plays. Wears his number, plays every game in his honor."

"Oh, that's good too. Really sad, though." She made another note, and I watched, wishing I could tell her my story. It was pretty compelling too, I thought, even though no one in the US had even heard of my country. But my history and my background were things I couldn't tell anyone. The only person in the states who had any idea who I really was was my Uncle Jericho. And he'd never tell a soul.

CHAPTER 10
LIZZY

PORTUGAL. NOT AN ISLAND.

THE EVENING with the prince ended up being fairly enjoyable. His ideas for a documentary weren't bad, either. If I let him help, I might actually have a chance of actually creating something to help the team out, something I hadn't really been planning on in the first place.

But if I kept him close, I could kill two birds with one stone, I figured. I could make sure he was safe, and I could start working on convincing him he needed to go home. The question was how exactly to do that without telling him who I was, admitting I knew who he was, or tipping him off to the very delicate state of his father's health—any of which could invalidate his claim to the throne.

"Call it a night?" I suggested, as he pushed away his drink.

He nodded. "Probably shouldn't have had that at all with a game tomorrow."

"I'll drive home?"

"It's my truck," he pointed out.

"I'll pick you up for the game."

He made a face. "You're quite a gentleman."

He didn't mean it that way, but the arrow sank deep. That was something I'd heard in different forms many times. Which was why I'd given up on dating. Men didn't want a woman who was every bit as tough or strong as they were. They didn't want a woman who could hold her own physically and verbally. They said they wanted an equal partner, but I had yet to find a man who didn't use my own strength against me somehow to make me feel like less of a woman.

"I'm sober," I told him.

"I mean, if you want to do math," he began. "I'm at about two-fifteen right now, and I don't think that wine counted as a real drink—"

"Then why do you drink it?" I couldn't help it. I was curious about the pink wine.

"Lizzy," he said, leaning forward slightly as if I should be able to figure this out for myself. "I got that for you."

"Oh," I said, understanding hitting as a laugh grew in my chest. "And I drank yours?"

"Yeah, you did," he laughed.

"I'm so sorry, I didn't know!" I couldn't stop laughing now, though I wasn't even sure why it was so funny. I'd accepted that the prince drank pink wine and just cataloged it as a quirk.

"I don't drink pink wine," I managed through a gasp. "Why would you assume that?"

He shook his head. "I shouldn't have. I'm sorry."

"For the record," I said. "There is good pink wine,

though. Just not white zinfandel. There's a tiny vineyard you've never heard of in an island country you've probably never heard of, and it makes the most amazing rosé."

"It's not Murdan Rosé, is it?" Declan raised an eyebrow.

Shit. I felt my heart drop into my stomach. I couldn't tell him I knew anything about our homeland. What had I been thinking? "No, what?"

The prince looked relieved, as if he'd brought up our country without thinking, just as I had.

"So what are you talking about?" We both stood and made our way toward the door.

"Sorry, what?" I had hoped he would just drop it.

"Good rose, you said. Tiny country?"

"Portugal," I managed to blurt. "They make great wine there."

Declan took my arm, turning me to face him. "Lizzy, I know athletes have a reputation for being ignorant… but I've heard of Portugal."

"Oh, well, yeah. I guess it's not that small of a country."

"Also…" Declan looked sheepish as he unlocked the truck. "Portugal is not an island, Lizzy."

"My bad," I managed, feeling a furious blush climb my cheeks.

I ended up letting the prince drive me back to my own car in the arena parking lot, but I followed him from a distance until I was sure he was home safe. And then I considered what a completely ridiculous situation I'd gotten myself into.

CHAPTER 11
DECK

DATING IS NOT A SOLUTION.

IN THE END, I had said goodnight to Lizzy in the parking lot, though I had an odd sensation I was being followed all the way home, and thought I might have seen her car out the window as I swept through the front room, readying for bed, but that would be insane. All I could figure was that my interest in her was starting to creep into areas it shouldn't.

For example, there was no earthly reason why I should've been out drinking the night before a game. But something about Lizzy brought out my worst instincts. Or, at least instincts I hadn't felt in a while.

I couldn't figure that particular woman out.

She was hot—no questions there.

She was capable—of what I wasn't quite sure. If I was honest, she seemed more built for athletics than for public relations. I wondered about her past—how had she gotten into this role in the first place? She'd explained, but it hadn't really answered the questions I still felt lingering around her.

But the bottom line was that she was also a pretty sizable distraction from hockey. And that was something I didn't need. That said, if I could help her make the team a household name, that would work to my advantage. If the world knew me as the most fascinating left winger in FHL hockey, then my position would be cemented here for the foreseeable future. And I needed to make it harder for Dad to come up with a reason to bring me home.

We'd won our game against the LA Cruisers, which was obviously a good thing. The roar of the crowd rang in my ears for hours after the final horn. It was one of those games where everything clicked. The pass from Stevens was pure perfection, slicing through the defense. I barely had time to think, just react—and the puck left my stick with a snap, finding the top corner behind their goalie. That goal tied it up, but the real highlight was the assist I set up for Remington in overtime. I fought off two defensemen in the corner, spun, and sent a blind backhand pass right to his tape. Watching him bury it, then the bench erupt, made everything else feel inconsequential. That was why I was here. For the game.

The next week at the rink, I did my best to keep my focus on the ice. Despite my offer to help her, I kind of avoided Lizzy. But it seemed like everyone else on the team was seeing plenty of her. And with every player that interacted with Lizzy and then returned to the team's locker room with reports, it became harder to ignore the irritating feeling growing in my gut.

I hadn't quite identified what that feeling was yet, but I knew it had to do with Lizzy, and I knew it had to do with me wanting to spend more time with her.

"She's so fucking hot, man," Van Porter reported, returning after practice one day to tell anyone who would listen about the interview he'd just done with Lizzy. "She's got this kind of quiet, demure thing happening. Like she wants someone to tell her what to do, you know?" He wiggled his eyebrows at this, and some of the other guys laughed salaciously.

I was squaring up on the guy before I even made a plan to do so. "She's here to work, Porter. Leave her alone." I was practically chest to chest with my younger teammate, and a few of the other guys stepped close in preparation to break us apart if needed.

"Whoa," Porter said, raising his hands and grinning. "Did you already get in there? Wouldn't want to step on your toes."

I leaned in closer, until he could probably feel my breath on his weasel face. "No one is 'getting in there,'" I assured him. "She's a professional. Don't touch her."

"Deck, man," Houstein was behind me now, a hand on my arm. "Everything's cool."

I forced a deep breath in and out and then stepped back, relaxing. "Yeah, okay."

Porter shook his head and exchanged a 'what the fuck' look with Corny, to his left.

I dressed quickly and left the locker room, forgoing my lengthy shower tonight. I wasn't in the mood.

Lizzy was still in the office she'd taken as her own when I walked by.

"Hey," I said, pausing in the doorway.

She looked up, a tight smile pulling her lips thin. She wore another of those tight sheath dresses that accentuated every muscle she had. She had plenty. What Porter didn't know, clearly, was that she could probably kick his ass. He hadn't seen her in that parking lot fight, but now that I thought more about it, it might've been her holding off two dudes to keep them from hurting me. And not the other way around. And that… Would be weird.

"Declan," she said, seeing me lingering in the doorway.

I'd ignored a message this morning that she was hoping to talk to me again, telling myself it made more sense to focus on hockey, and kind of worried about my own less-than-professional interest in her. I told myself I should forget that I'd offered to help her with her documentary. Because honestly? If I spent too much time with Lizzy, I might act on my feelings. And the last thing I needed was to piss off Coach. But if the guys were getting into her space, maybe she really did need me.

"Sorry I haven't been around to help. It was a busy week."

She nodded.

"I should have more time now though," I said. Nothing in my schedule had changed at all. But something else had. I could acknowledge that what I'd felt was jealousy when Porter had talked about her that way. "So fill me in. How are things going?"

She waved toward a chair to one side of the room.

"Things are about where they were before. The guys don't really want to open up to me, you know? They want to talk about hockey."

"Go figure," I laughed. "Yeah, we're a single-minded bunch, I guess."

She raised an eyebrow and let out a slow breath. "Well, I may not be the most experienced at this, but I suspect a movie with a bunch of guys talking about how they wrap their sticks and their favorite way to check another player against the boards probably isn't going to be super compelling."

"Nope."

"I need a way to get inside," she said. "Make them trust me, I guess."

I nodded. "I have an idea," I told her. It was a terrible idea if you were me… But I knew it would probably help Lizzy. And I couldn't exactly pretend that I didn't have my own motivations. The problem was that my own motivations would possibly get me in trouble.

"Let's hear it. I'm drowning here." She sank into the chair across from me and crossed her legs, and for a minute I was completely distracted by the bulge of her calf muscle as she jiggled her toes, making her high heel flick back and forth.

I took a deep breath, partially to keep my brain from actually thinking about what was about to come out of my mouth. "Date me," I suggested.

Her eyebrows rose nearly into her hairline. "What??"

CHAPTER 12

LIZZY

NO "FUN STUFF"

I WASN'T sure I'd heard the prince correctly.

I stared at him. "What?"

"Date me," he said again with a little shrug, as if this wasn't out of the blue and completely random.

"I might not date much, but I'm pretty sure this isn't how it works, Declan."

He chuckled and rubbed one hand through his wavy dark locks, stirring something in me I did my best to ignore. "Not real dating. Fake dating." Then he laughed and pointed at me and said, "I can't believe you thought I really wanted to date you."

"Ouch."

His face fell. "I mean I would totally date you… I mean, I can't date you. Not that you are interested in dating me. Boy this is not going well… What I'm trying to say, is that we can't date."

"If we can't date, then why would you suggest we date?"

"Yeah," he said. "This isn't coming out quite the way I

thought it would. Not that I thought a lot about it actually. What I'm suggesting is fake dating. We just pretend to date. None of the fun stuff, you know, none of that… Never mind."

The slow blush climbing the prince's face made me question how fit he really was to sit the throne. He wasn't proving himself to be especially well spoken or eloquent. But none of that was my concern. I had a job to do, and being closer to the prince would help me do it. But pretending to be linked to him romantically whether or not we did any of the "fun stuff," would be a bit of a gray area. Sure, I had navigated gray areas before. Like when I had to take out a particularly nasty general on the borders of a rainforest that may or may not have been cleared for operations. But this was different.

I shook my head. More acting was the last thing I needed here. I was making zero progress on convincing the prince to go home, and if I didn't begin really working on this documentary, I was going to lose my proximity. "I think this is a bad plan."

"Why?"

"Explain how pretending to date would get me better access to the team."

Now Declan leaned back in his chair, crossing his arms over his chest, making every muscle pop. "I'm a respected player here, known to avoid meaningless hookups. If I date someone, people know we're serious. If I bring her around the team, it makes it clear she's trustworthy."

I couldn't help myself. "How many of these trustworthy women have you brought around in the past?"

A half-smile lifted one side of his mouth. "One."

"And where is she?"

The smile disappeared. "She deserved more. I let her go."

That was interesting. Declan would never be able to tell anyone he dated who he really was. Would that ruin his chances for real love here in the United States? Women asked for honesty and trust—and he couldn't offer it. Maybe that was something I could use to my advantage…

"I'm sorry," I offered. But I wasn't sorry. If Declan had been in love with someone, that would have made my job doubly difficult. I was still considering knocking the big oaf out and shoving him onto a private jet back home.

Also, I didn't like the idea of Declan being in love. But I wasn't going to explore that. Not now.

"Can't we just strike up a friendship?" I asked.

He frowned. "Guys like me don't have a lot of time for friends outside the team during the season."

"But you make time for women?"

"There are… obvious advantages to women," he said, and that deep blush crept up his cheeks beneath the stubble covering his jaw.

"Oh really?"

"Don't make me be lewd. You know what I mean."

"You're referring to the 'fun stuff' you mentioned a minute ago?" I was beginning to enjoy making the prince uncomfortable.

"Just date me," he said again, waiting for my answer. "We'll get you where you need to be to make a really excellent movie. The guys will trust you, and then we both win."

It made little sense. The king wouldn't like it. I had every reason to say no. "I don't know."

"That is not a no," he said, rising and giving me the grin he'd worn since he was a kid, the one that made me feel like we were children again, hiding out in the little-used throne room at the palace. "Team dinner tomorrow night at Teakhouse Tavern. We'll debut there."

"So soon?"

"No time like tomorrow," he said, pulling his bag back to his shoulder and turning to the door.

"I think the saying is no time like the present," I said.

"Whatever."

And just like that, the prince and I were dating. Fake dating. But I wasn't nearly as sure about anything as he seemed to be.

Deck headed out and I shadowed him to make sure he got home safely. Then I headed to my own apartment to mull over the choices I'd made and the lack of progress I had to show for them.

And finally, when I couldn't procrastinate it any longer, I picked up the phone to make my report to the palace.

"Lizzy, hello darling," came the Queen's tired voice when the private line picked up.

"Your Majesty. Is everything all right?"

"No. Erik's had a spell."

The king.

"Oh dear, will he be all right?"

"He's fine for now, but I want my husband to live his final days secure in the knowledge that Declan will pick up where he left off. We really need you to hurry, Lizzy. Bring my son home."

"I will do my best," I said. I dropped my eyes shut, suddenly exhausted. I paused, knowing I needed to tell the palace about the attempt on Declan's life, but just as I was about to speak, the Queen sighed again. The sound carried so much sadness, so much exhaustion… I considered whether she could bear this additional load right now.

No, it was my duty. I might be an empathetic human being, but this was my job.

I cleared my throat, but the Queen spoke before I could get the words out.

"I imagine we don't have long," the Queen said, and the sadness and misery in her voice pulled at something inside me. For all of their formality, and sheer regality, the king and queen had always been clearly in love. I envied them that, and I could only imagine how difficult it was for the Queen to watch her husband suffer.

CHAPTER 13
DECK

YOU WANT ME TO SIGN... WHAT?

AS SOON AS the suggestion was out, I'd known it was a mistake of gigantic proportions. I couldn't date Lizzy—there was the obvious no fraternization policy I'd have to deal with now. The coach would not be understanding…

I did feel somewhat smug knowing that no one else on the team would bother now, thanks to my little plan, but there was another thing I wasn't as eager to admit.

I liked her.

I barely knew her, but I liked her. She reminded me of someone—of home in some way. Not in the "do your duty" kind of way I'd run away from, but of the really amazing things I'd loved about my home country. Or at least the things I'd loved as a kid—the warm salt-washed days on the beach, the crystal blue water of the ocean, the sweeping grandeur of the sky above us… I'd had my brother and my best friend Eliza back in those days.

But those days were long gone. Lizzy was her own

person. And she was a person I was having trouble not thinking about.

I found myself distracted even when she wasn't around, pondering the way her strong legs created incredible curves in the pencil skirts she sometimes favored, the way her calf muscles popped when she wore those high heels. I thought about how she'd looked at me across the table that first night, like she knew something, like she could see something I'd kept hidden from the world.

It was impossible, of course. She couldn't know me any better than anyone else had since I was a kid. Part of the agreement I'd made in coming to play hockey involved hiding my real identity. Sure, there were plenty of psychobabble gurus who would probably point out that stuffing down an entire part of your identity and refusing to acknowledge it was unhealthy for the psyche… But if that was what it took to earn my freedom, it was okay.

Mostly.

I missed my family. The monthly calls I had with Mom and Dad were full of small talk and false politeness. I barely knew them anymore. And Dad had sounded odd last time we'd spoken. Tired.

My brother was a whole other story. Lambert had pushed the limits of his position for years. Since the time I'd left, really. He'd begun toying with drugs—not a great option for anyone, let alone an eighteen-year-old. He'd been to rehab several times since then, and my parents were exhausted by his reputation as the Playboy Prince. I had always figured he would settle down once he was king.

I sighed. In a weird way, I missed Lambert. My big

brother had been my best friend. He'd understood why I wanted to leave, though. He'd encouraged me to go. But then he'd… well, I didn't like to think about it. The timing could lead one to feel guilty about everything. He'd been fine until I'd fled to America.

But we were individuals. His choices were just that. His own. Not that he had the option to walk away. I guess that was the real difference. And there was a certain amount of guilt inherent in my understanding of that fact. A whole buttload of guilt, really.

And my choice to let the team think that Lizzy and I were dating?

Mine.

I guessed both princes were poor decision makers sometimes.

At four-thirty the next day, I pulled on my nicest board shorts and my favorite T-shirt, grabbed a Wilcox Wombats ball cap and put on my sunglasses. I had a date to pick up.

Lizzy had given me her address—she lived in a tall condo building I was surprised she could afford on a PR salary, but then again, I knew very little about her family situation or her past. Maybe she came from royalty too.

Ha.

As she'd directed, I let the doorman know who I was, and he called up for me.

"She'll be right down," the guy told me, giving me a wide smile.

"Thanks," I said.

There was an awkward pause while I waited for Lizzy, and the man kept smiling at me. I glanced his way again, feeling incredibly uncomfortable since it was just the two of us in the small lobby and his attention was so completely focused on me.

"I'm a fan," he said after another long beat of staring and smiling.

"Thanks, man," I said, hoping that would be it.

More staring. More smiling.

"Did you want me to like, sign anything?" I asked. It wasn't my usual interaction with fans, but I wasn't usually in such a confined space with someone refusing to look away.

"Oh, that would be amazing," he said, and to my horror, he peeled up the top half of his uniform and presented me with a very broad, very pale gut.

"You want me to sign your… stomach?"

The man grinned harder and nodded, his eyes sparkling as if this was the best day of his life.

I took the Sharpie sitting on the counter and knelt to get myself into position.

And then the elevator door dinged, and I heard someone step into the lobby, catching me on my knees in front of a partially clad doorman.

Lizzy's gasp came immediately. "Declan?"

This was not exactly the impression I'd hoped to give Lizzy on our first official fake date.

CHAPTER 14
LIZZY

THE PRINCE JUMPED to his feet and Arnold tucked his uniform back around his sizable middle. I stared at them both.

"He asked for an autograph," Declan said, a blush turning his handsome face pink.

"I.. sorry, ma'am. I forgot myself." Arnold couldn't hold my gaze. And for good reason. He was an unofficial member of the King's Guard, and the behavior I'd just witnessed was a fireable offense. He could be excommunicated for such disrespect to a member of the royal family.

I shook my head. I couldn't blame him for being overcome, so close to his prince.

I felt a little overcome myself every time I was caught in the glow of Declan's blue-eyed gaze, whenever he put a hand to my low back as we walked together into a room.

And now, standing there in a pair of long shorts and a T-shirt that proclaimed that "surely not everyone was kung-fu fighting," I was battling some kind of chemical reaction inside my body that I was powerless to control.

"It's fine. Should we go?" I asked the prince.

"Yeah. See ya," he said to Arnold, who still looked frightened and ashamed. Good. I'd have to talk to him later. He'd been appointed as a cover—to keep an eye on the building and report anything suspicious.

As we climbed into Declan's truck, he tried to explain. "I wasn't doing anything weird, you know. I just needed better leverage. His tummy was so low."

"I'd rather not discuss it," I said.

"Oh, yeah. Totally." He pulled the big truck away from the curb. "You ready for this?"

"Not even a little bit," I said. Agreeing to pretend to date was not part of my plan. The only reason I hadn't refused was because there was a good chance that this access to Declan would allow me to begin to gain his confidence. Once he'd told me who he was, I could be honest with him. It would make everything easier. In the meantime, I had to keep trying to figure out how to make him decide to go home while pretending I had no idea who he was. It was impossible.

We'd barely left the curb in front of my building when Declan pulled the car over and looked at me. "Lizzy," he said, and his voice carried a low, sexy tone that pulled at something inside me. I looked over at him.

"Yeah?"

"We don't have to do this. I would never make you do something you're not comfortable with. I really was just trying to help," he said. "That, and..." he trailed off.

I shook my head lightly. "That and what?" There was something in the way he was looking at me, the way his gaze dropped to my lips for a second and then caught my eyes again. My stomach twisted and heat flashed through me.

"If I'm honest," he said, his voice so low it had me clenching my thighs together.

Dammit.

He rubbed a hand across the back of his neck, gave a deep, rumbling chuckle. "Well, look. You're gorgeous, which I'm sure you know. And maybe I should have just asked you out for real, except I'm really not supposed to get involved with anyone who works for the team, and I was 99 percent sure you'd turn me down."

"I would," I said, still struggling to get my reactions to him under control. In the small cab of the truck, the prince suddenly seemed so huge, so overwhelmingly masculine. What would it be like to succumb to all that…man?

"So I went with fake," he said, nodding as if he'd known I would say that. "But just because I find you attractive doesn't mean I can't be a total gentleman."

I struggled not to blurt out that a gentleman was suddenly the last thing I wanted him to be. "Okay."

"I'm attracted to you. But I'm not a caveman," he went on. "I want to help you get the team's trust. And I can do that without acting on… whatever… this is." He gestured between us. "Only… do you… am I nuts here? Do you not feel this thing between us?"

I did. I felt it winding through me, pushing me to move closer to him, to press myself against him, to let his heat and his overwhelming masculinity take over. To see what kinds of "fun stuff" the prince might have in mind…

But that was definitely not what I was here for, and I couldn't tell the king that I'd seduced the prince. Forget my fake PR job, that would have me stripped of every commendation I'd earned.

"I'm sorry, Declan. I just don't feel anything," I managed. I thought it was pretty convincing too, if you didn't notice the grip my fingernails had on the leather of Declan's car seat.

He blew out a breath. "Okay then. Good thing I went ahead and humiliated myself early. Now that that's out of the way, let's get to this dinner, yeah?"

"Yeah," I said. "But Declan? I don't know that anyone would believe that I would accompany you to a team event as your date so soon after meeting. Especially now that I know that would be breaking a rule."

"Yeah… Of course." Declan looked sheepish as he turned his eyes back to the windshield. "Then…we're just friends," he said, and something in me sagged a bit as he said it. "Nothing wrong with that."

As he pulled away from the curb and my body began to relax once again, I felt something else—disappointment. I liked being the center of his attention. Not only did it appeal to the woman I had become, but it spoke to the kid I once was, the poor girl who had a prince's full attention and affection. I missed that feeling, that certainty that someone saw me for who I really was… And I wanted more.

But more was something I couldn't have.

The atmosphere in the Teakhouse Tavern was very different than it had been the night after the attack when I learned of the prince's affinity for pink wine. The team was here, gathered around several tables and impossible to miss. The mood was boisterous and fun; teammates laughing heartily, slapping each other on the back, and generally behaving like little boys whose parents were sitting at the grown-ups table and looking the other way.

Declan and I walked in and the noise level dropped significantly. Heads began to turn, each set of eyes taking in the two of us together before each face tried to mask a surprised expression.

"There you are." One man stood from the head of the table, and I recognized Coach Merritt. He did not look especially happy to see either one of us, and I gathered that Declan was late. "And hello," he said to me looking confused about my presence at the team dinner. "You're the PR person, right?" The coach's face was somewhere between irritated and confused, and I sensed that maybe coming with Declan had been a big mistake.

"Coach, hey," Declan said. "I thought Lizzy here would benefit from getting a real feel for the team dynamic. Maybe pick up some great stuff she can use to help promote us."

"Yeah," Sly Remington called out. "She can tell the world about how many cannolis you can put away after an entire tray of lasagna, Deck."

"Or maybe she can post an Insta reel of Solamentes snarfing Pepsi out his nose again," John Samuels suggested.

"It was one time," Mario Solamentes said, looking hurt. "And that was Rock's fault. He made me laugh."

"Can't help that I'm fuckin' hilarious," Rock Stevens chimed in, rocking back in his chair until he was at a precarious angle.

"That's enough!" The coach roared. "Well, you're here now. Might as well sit down. And Deck, don't think I didn't notice that you're fifteen minutes late as usual."

I followed Declan to two open spots at the far end of the table, somewhat relieved not to be sitting near the coach.

"So these team dinners, what is the purpose exactly?" I asked.

Declan pulled out my chair for me and I sat, John Samuels on one side of me and another player I hadn't met yet directly across from me. Though I had asked the question to Declan, John leaned in.

"The idea is to help us bond. So that we gel as a team on the ice and off the ice."

"And does that work?" I asked. I thought about the dinners I'd had with other operatives to work for the King's Guard. Generally those dinners were full of one-upmanship and suspicion. There were usually cherry opportunities on the line, we all knew it, and no one liked to lose. It was part of what made a good agent, that sense of competition and the desire to kick anyone's ass.

"I don't know," said the guy sitting across from me. "They did make me like you better, Sammy."

Declan leaned in. "Not everybody was a big fan of the

new goalie when he stepped up last year," he explained. "Harry here was a big Mizzoni groupie."

"I wasn't a groupie," the man Declan had called Harry said indignantly. I guessed he must be Harry Foranian, one of the centers on the team. He went on, trying to explain. "Mizzoni was just, he was like…"

"You had a poster of him on your wall like all the rest of us did," said Declan.

"Yeah, because he was a legend," John said.

Declan whispered in my ear again sending a shiver across my skin. "Mizzoni was totally a legend. I had a poster of him too. Retired last year."

"All right you two, let's get your drinks and food ordered and get on with it," the coach yelled from his end of the table. Coach Merritt, though clearly good at his job based on the team's record, left a bit to be desired in terms of congeniality. He had been welcoming enough initially, but it was clear he wasn't excited about my presence here, which made it even harder to do a job I had no idea how to do in the first place.

Declan and I ordered sodas and food, having come in behind the rest of the team. And as soon as we finished ordering, the coach began yelling again.

"All right yahoos, we leave day after tomorrow for North Carolina. You know we'll be facing the Vikings, and those guys are pretty damn good. They've got that aggressive forecheck, and last time they pinned us deep and forced bad turnovers. Their wingers—especially #17—love to crash the net hard, so our D needs to box them out early and clear those rebounds. And watch their center on the power play—he's got that quick one-timer from the right circle, and we gave him way too much space last game. We tighten up, play smart in our zone, and keep our heads up on the breakout, and I know we can take this one."

Declan and the rest of the team were cheering and nodding as the coach delivered this confusing jumble of terms and directions, but they all seemed to understand what he was saying. The part I was focused on was the travel.

I knew Declan would be traveling with the team during the season, and it worried me. There had been one attempt on his life already, and the team schedule was public knowledge. It would be much easier to get to him in some unguarded hotel somewhere than it would be here where I had eyes on him at all times. For a moment, I forgot to play the demure PR rep, and words were coming out of my mouth before I had thought them through.

"What kind of security do you guys use while you travel? And where will you be staying?"

Every single head at the table turned to look at me and half of the mouths dropped open. Oops.

"Security?" The coach asked, tilting his head at me.

"Yeah, I mean… I just wonder how you deal with all of the fans?" I scrambled trying to cover my error in some way that might relate my security question to public relations.

"Well I guess you'll be finding out," the coach said. "Since the owner told me in no uncertain terms that you were going to be traveling with the team."

I had suggested to the king that I would need to travel with the team, and he had told me he would make this request to the owner. However, the owner had not liked the idea, and I had thought that it wasn't happening. It was something I had intended to worry about when the moment came. Now that the moment was here, it seemed that there was less to worry about.

"Oh, right. Sure. That's good." I was not sounding entirely professional.

"Now that we've got the PR side of things buttoned up, let's talk about strategy against the Vikings." The coach continued.

For the rest of dinner, the team discussed their last few games against the Vikings, naming certain players, and using several very colorful descriptions of their abilities. It had never occurred to me that a hockey player might skate like a turnstile or a Dollar Store Gretzky, but evidently those were things that were possible.

When the game talk had concluded and all the plates had been cleared, the coach got up and left rather unceremoniously. He probably said goodbye to the players sitting next to him at the table, but he didn't wish anyone else a good evening. Things were done very differently here in Wilcox than they were inside the palace, that was for sure. I glanced at Declan to see how he handled the lack of etiquette, but he'd been in the states for a long time now, surrounded by athletes, who obviously didn't put as much stock in the rules of society as those he'd been raised with did.

"So," John Samuels asked me. "How's it coming? The whole making the Wombats a household name thing?"

I was about to speak when Declan spoke in my place. "It's going to be awesome, man!"

I glanced at him and he winked at me, sending a shiver that I did not want down my spine. Knowing that Declan felt something for me, or at least was attracted to me, had only made my job more complicated. Because his attraction, coupled with my own undeniable attraction for him, could be explosive. I didn't need the prince winking at me, fake dating me, or otherwise complicating my efforts to protect him and convince him to come home. And this somewhat unwarranted faith he seemed to have in my public relations abilities was also unsettling.

"She's putting together this really amazing movie, you guys," Declan said.

"A movie?" Mario Solamentes asked, looking suddenly interested.

"Well, it's just one idea we had. I mean, I had," I said.

"I think a movie could be really awesome," said John Samuels. "Won't you need some kind of like anchoring story?"

"Yeah, that's right," Declan interrupted. "I was going to ask you guys, do any of you have a blind sister?"

The men around us exchanged confused looks and I narrowed my eyes at the prince, not that he noticed. I turned back to the other men. "I do need some kind of centering story," I said. "I thought I might try to build something around the sport of hockey being a unifier."

"What does that even mean?" Solamentes asked.

"I'm not sure yet," I said, thinking. "But in my head, it's something about everyone being from a different background, coming from different parts of the world, even, and finding that you're all part of a family because of this game you play, this team."

I looked at Declan to see a strange expression on his face. His eyes slid toward me and narrowed slightly, and for a second I worried if I had gone a little bit too far. But I needed to start building a connection to his real life to give him the ability to tell me who he really was.

CHAPTER 15
DECK

NICE SCONCES...

WE TRAVELED to North Carolina a couple of days later to face the Vikings. When we got there, the team went to practice at the rink in the early afternoon, and we were all back at the hotel at a reasonable hour to get enough sleep before the game. As soon as I had the key to my room, Lizzy was at my side.

"Didn't you get your own key?" I asked her. "Not that I would mind sharing..."

"Yes, I got my own room."

She still stayed by my side as I exited the elevator and moved down the hallway toward my room at the end of the hall. When I opened the door, she stepped inside ahead of me, nearly pushing me out of the way like she just couldn't wait to see the place.

"Lizzy," I said. "What are you doing?"

She gave me a funny look but didn't answer me, and then proceeded to walk around the room, running her hands under things, lifting up the fabric beneath the bed, looking inside the lamps, and doing a very comprehensive visual search of every nook and cranny of the room.

"What are you looking for?" I asked her.

"Nothing," she said.

I could think of no reason why the PR rep for the team would need to carefully investigate my entire room.

"Lose something?" I asked knowing this was impossible since she'd never been here before.

Lizzy stood up straight, her shoulders tensing. "Um, no, sorry. It's just… I heard this was a super nice hotel. So I was just checking things out. I wanted to see if your room is exactly like my room, or if maybe every room is different. Because that would be neat, right?"

"Right..." I answered, not quite buying it. "Neat. Do you want me to come to your room now and feel all the fabric to see if it's the same?"

"That would be ridiculous," said Lizzy.

She stared at me for a bit longer, something unreadable passing through her eyes as she did. It was pretty early, and I didn't need to go to bed for a couple of hours, but I didn't have a whole lot else to do, either.

"You have plans for the night?" I asked her. "Now that you've evaluated the sconces and whatnot?"

"Not really," she said. "I was gonna maybe watch some television and go to bed."

"Me too," I said. "Would you wanna maybe hang out a little bit? Just as friends, of course."

"I... okay."

Lizzy walked to the couch at the side of the room and sat down, looking around herself nervously. I grabbed a couple of waters from the minibar, handed one to her, and sat across from her.

"Where are you from, Lizzy?"

"Why do you ask?"

"Well, if we're gonna be friends, I feel like I should know a little bit about you. So where did you grow up?"

"Nowhere around here."

She wouldn't meet my eyes, and I got the sense that there was something she was hiding. I couldn't imagine why she would hide where she grew up—but then I realized maybe it was a place she wasn't proud of.

"That's okay," I said. "Were you happy as a kid? Did you have a good family? Do you keep in touch with them?"

"That's a lot of questions, Declan."

"You don't have to answer them. I'm just trying to get to know you."

The weird thing was, I really did want her to answer them. There was something about Lizzy that felt so familiar, like there was some thread of commonality that we shared that I couldn't put my finger on. And while I understood that nothing could ever happen between us—at least not while she was working for the team—some part of me felt like she might understand me in a way that other women had never been able to.

Of course, that was insane, because I could never tell any woman the truth about who I really was or where I was from. That was something I had accepted a long time ago, and the one serious relationship I had tried had failed spectacularly for that very reason. I had chosen my freedom, and freedom meant being alone. For me, at least.

"I grew up happy," said Lizzy. "My mom loved me. I didn't see my dad a lot, but that was okay. I didn't have any brothers or sisters."

Lizzy hesitated, and there was something in her eyes I couldn't quite identify.

"But I did have a best friend. Who felt a lot like a brother when we were young."

Lizzy's voice was slow as she said these words, hesitant, like there was something she was divulging that she wasn't sure she should tell me. "What about you?"

"I do have a brother," I told her. "We used to be pretty close. But we're not now, and I feel like that's my fault in a lot of ways."

"Your fault how?"

I lifted a shoulder. "It's complicated, but I guess you could say I kind of abandoned him. There was a job," I searched for a way to tell her what had gone down. "It wasn't ever supposed to be mine because, well, it just wasn't. It was always going to be his. But it's a really hard job, and he didn't really want it. And so when I left to pursue my dreams, I think maybe he was kind of jealous." My heart twisted at the thought of Lambert and how he'd opted to handle the pressure and disappointment. And at the guilt I always felt about it.

"That must be hard," Lizzy said. She nodded in sympathy and then went on. "I don't have any siblings, but I've seen how those relationships operate. I feel like there's a lot of expectation between siblings. And that would be kind of difficult."

"Yeah, maybe that's it."

I thought about Lambert back at home. Abandoned, because I left him there. Abandoned to rule a kingdom, sure, which is something most people might want. Or think that they want. But I had abandoned him all the same. Because I selfishly wanted to pursue my own dreams, and he was kind enough to encourage me to do it.

"I didn't grow up with money," Lizzy volunteered suddenly. "I grew up with a tough mom, who had to make her own way. And so she made me tough, I think."

"Yeah, I saw that the other night in the parking lot," I reminded her.

Lizzy's gaze dropped to her lap for a second as she inspected the top of her water bottle, toying with it before meeting my eyes again.

"It has made things a little bit difficult," she said.

"What has? Being independent?"

"Yeah," she hesitated. "But also... men aren't always looking for a woman who can put them on their ass."

I grinned. I couldn't help it. It was exactly what I had thought the first time I saw her. And for me, that was my catnip. I didn't want a shy, demure toothpick of a blonde who I could blow over with one misplaced high five. I wanted a woman who could hold her own, who knew what she wanted and wasn't afraid to try to get it. I wanted a woman like Lizzy.

If, of course, I could have a woman at all. Which, as had already been established, I could not.

"Well, that's ridiculous," I told her. "And any guy who is afraid of a woman who can handle herself doesn't deserve a woman like you in the first place."

I watched, intrigued, as an adorable blush climbed Lizzy's neck, her dark hair hanging around her face as she looked down at the top of the water bottle again, a tiny smile pulling her full lips just slightly wider. I liked that I could make her blush, that I could make her smile. If nothing else, Lizzy deserved to hear that she was gorgeous —and that I appreciated her ability to kick my ass.

Suddenly Lizzy stood, putting her water bottle on the coffee table between us.

"Well, I should go."

I followed her to the door of my room. As she opened it, I stepped in front of her for a second, wanting to keep her just for a moment.

"Don't forget to let me know," I told her.

"Let you know what?"

"Whether your room has the same high-end fabrics and appointments as mine does."

Lizzy grinned at me and then turned and walked toward the elevators.

I wished that I could go with her. Wished that we could be something more than friends. Wished... I didn't know exactly what.

The next morning, we had a quick practice, lunch as a team, and then headed to the arena for the game.

Lizzy stayed mostly in the background, but I did see her asking some of the guys questions and recording things on her phone. I hoped she was finding a solid idea for the movie.

Joey, John Samuels's fiancée, had come along on the trip too. I had noticed her and Lizzy talking a bit on the plane and hoped that would make things more comfortable for Lizzy—having a friend. As we took the ice at the Viking's arena, I spotted them sitting together, their heads close as the Wombats were called out. And I watched her face as they announced my name, a little thrill spiking inside me as she shot a fist into the air and cheered for me.

Of course, no amount of cheering could fix the mess I made out there. I had the puck on my stick with twenty seconds left, a clean shot to tie it up, and I sent it right into the goalie's crest like a damn warm-up drill. Then I got caught deep on the backcheck, left my guy wide open, and watched—helpless—as he buried the empty-netter to seal the loss. Just like that, game over.

I avoided looking up at Lizzy and Joey as I skated off the ice, and I was betting Samuels wasn't too excited about Coach's take on the final play either, since it had lost us the game. It was my fault, not John's, but that wouldn't stop him beating himself up over letting that one through.

"Hey," Corny said, moving up to my side in the locker room where I was busily avoiding all eye contact and beating myself up. "Coulda happened to anyone."

"Thanks."

His words didn't make me feel better. If anything, they just made me feel shittier. These guys were my teammates, my brothers. But I guess that was what I did—let my brothers down.

As we gathered in front of the hotel that night to load the bus and head back to the airport, I was doing my best to halt the constant replay going in my mind. I'd been avoiding Lizzy too, though I wasn't sure exactly why.

Maybe I just didn't want her to have to hide her disappointment at my playing.

I'd just stowed my stuff under the bus, when my stomach gave a groan. I glanced around, seeing that we'd be loading up for at least another ten minutes.

"Hey," I told Derek Reed. "I'm gonna run to the convenience store I saw on the next block. Be right back."

Derek looked around, probably for the coach. "You better be fast," he told me.

My usually snarky retort was unavailable. I couldn't even make jokes about being speedy and reliable at that moment. "I'll be right back. Don't let the bus leave."

"Dude…"

I turned, heading in the direction I'd seen the shop, and half jogged to the convenience store. It turned out to be more like six blocks instead of one, but I figured I had time to grab a chocolate milk and a bag of Raisinets.

As I ducked through the door, I had a weird feeling like someone was following me, a feeling that didn't get better when I spotted two burly dudes dressed mostly in black stepping through the door right behind me. I headed to one side of the store, seeking out the milk, but I could feel the guys in the store behind me, like their attention was trained on me.

I pulled the milk out and spun, only to find one of the guys standing directly behind me. I nearly ran right into him as I moved toward the candy aisle.

"Sorry, dude," I muttered. Seriously, what was his deal?

As I searched for the Raisinets, the guy stepped into the narrow aisle to one side of me while his buddy came in from the other direction. Big guy number one had a scar running along one cheek, though I was doing my best not to stare. He moved close—a little closer than I thought was necessary for a fellow candy-lover, and I stepped to the other side, practically running into big guy number two.

"You guys big sugar fiends too?" I asked, wishing they'd back up a bit.

Big guy number one lifted one side of his lips in what might have been a smile but looked more like a snarl, revealing that he was missing a few teeth.

"You play hockey, man?" Maybe these were just fans, looking for an autograph? People got weird when they met their sports idols.

"No," he growled, his hand moving to his belt in a way that set the hair on the back of my neck standing on end.

His hand lifted the black fabric of his shirt and I saw something glint at his belt just as the door jingled and half my team poured inside. The guy dropped his hand.

"Deck, man, there you are!" Rock Stevens moved to my side, practically shoulder-checking big guy number two without seeming to notice. He reached down and scooped up three Twix bars before considering and then reaching for one more. He actually turned and offered one to big guy number one, who looked irritated by the sudden influx of Wombat players.

"Guys, we need to bounce. Right now!" Panther Aspen swept down the candy aisle, pushing Rock and I ahead of him to pay. We practically threw money at the poor girl behind the register, apologizing as we hauled ass out the door and back down to the bus.

"Coach mad?" I asked Rock as we jogged.

"Nah, he said if I got him a Twix, we'd be good."

"Yeah, you'll be good," I grumbled. "Hey, did you see those two dudes in there?"

"Not really, why?"

"I dunno, they were just acting kinda weird. Set my Spidey senses blinging."

He laughed. "We could definitely take those guys."

"The ones you didn't see?"

"Half a hockey team can take pretty much anyone," he said. And then he slowed to a walk and grabbed my arm, halting me. "And even when you blow a block, we're still gonna have your back, man. Happens to all of us."

I nodded, hoping my face didn't show quite how much I'd needed to hear that.

After what felt like hours, we were settled on the jet, which the team chartered whenever possible to make the demanding travel a little easier.

I tried not to look too happy when Lizzy took the seat next to me.

Soon after take off, I pulled out my chocolate raisins and caught her eyeballing them.

"You want a few?"

She shook her head, sending that ponytail slipping over her shoulder again and sparking the same fantasy I'd been having since we'd met.

"No thanks. They remind me of rabbit poop."

"Rabbits are super cute," I reminded her.

"Poop is not."

"Fair point."

Lizzy didn't mention the game, and I was glad for it. Most of the plane was silent as we headed back to Virginia, leaving me to ponder my poor playing in relative peace. Things turned around a little when, about halfway through the flight, Lizzy's head slipped from the seat back and landed on my shoulder.

For the rest of the flight, I did everything in my power not to move. Having her so close I could smell the floral scent of her shampoo helped soothe the hurts I'd gathered that night. Feeling the warmth of her cheek against my shoulder gave me some kind of misplaced hope for something. And for the extent of the flight home? I wasn't going to question it.

We were taxiing toward the gate when my phone vibrated with a text. Lizzy awoke when the plane touched down, removing her head from my shoulder without mentioning anything about having fallen asleep there. I reached into my pocket for the phone, missing the feel of her so close to me.

I was shocked to see one line from my brother.

Lambert: Call me please.

CHAPTER 16
LIZZY

DON'T DISCOUNT THE BUTT.

FOR THE NEXT few days after returning from North Carolina, I spent a lot of time with Joey Baxter, John Samuels's fiancée. She was fun and energetic and, she introduced me to some of the other wives and girlfriends. For some reason, very excited about my PR assignment for the team. John himself was already a PR draw, given that he was the youngest starting goalie in the FHL.

"You know, wombats are actually super interesting," Joey said one night as I sat across the table from her at the Teakhouse, a scotch in front of me. Declan and John were reviewing tapes from the North Carolina game, hoping to overcome whatever issues had flagged them and led to the loss. I'd slipped a tracker onto Declan's truck, and could see that he was still at John's house, which had been part of my original security evaluation when I'd arrived. It was as secure as a private home could be. I hoped John used his security system when he was home. Or at least locked his doors. People could be so careless.

"What do you mean by interesting?" I asked, sipping my scotch.

Joey leaned her head to one side, her eyes widening. "Oh my gosh, there's so much."

I scrunched my nose at her. Wombats had really never crossed my radar prior to this assignment. As far as I knew, they were some sort of exotic marsupial native to Australia. I hadn't come across any in my lifetime, and I still didn't understand how a Virginia-based hockey team had come to be named for such a strange animal.

I supposed having a new friend meant I should humor her quirks. Maybe affection for marsupials was one of Joey's. "Why don't you tell me about them?"

"Well, for one thing, they are adorable."

Joey pulled out her phone and showed me a bunch of images of squat, fat, furry animals with big dark noses and very long claws. I had to admit, they were cute. They looked kind of snuggly, and one video seemed to suggest they could be trained to do laundry.

"They are cute," I admitted. "But cute does not necessarily mean interesting, Joey."

"Right. But how about this? Did you know that their poop is cube-shaped?"

"Why would I know that?"

"Well, it is. And wombats use their cube-shaped poop to build towers, mark territory, and attract mates."

She was giving me a look after this statement that told me I should be extremely impressed by animals who build towers out of their own feces, but I was struggling to feel much of anything about this odd fact. Maybe a vague sense of disgust.

"Fine, I have more." Joey smiled and then gave me a look that seemed to say she was very determined to sway my opinion of wombats.

I waved my hand for her to proceed. "By all means."

"Wombats. Have. Killer. Butts." She pronounced every word of this statement with exaggerated emphasis and then stared at me.

"Excuse me?"

"Killer butts." She waited, saying nothing else.

"Joey, I'm gonna need a little more."

"Their butts are how they kill predators."

A raft of images came to mind as I tried to imagine how these small, fat, furry creatures could kill anything with their butts. But I didn't have to consider the options for long because Joey was pulling up a video on her phone. Moments later, I watched as a big, fat wombat fled from a fox. It dove into its burrow and then squatted down, waiting for the predator to stick its head inside. When the silly fox did, the wombat did the craziest upward twerk I'd ever seen and smashed the fox's skull against the roof of its burrow.

As it did this, Joey yelled. "BAM!" A nearby couple shot us dirty looks as the woman leaned across the table to blot the man's sleeve with a napkin after he'd been startled enough to spill his drink.

"Wow," I said. That was actually very impressive. I had never considered how wombats might take on predators, but now I had a healthy respect for them—and for the power of the butt in general.

"OK," I said to Joey. "That is super impressive. But it doesn't actually help me with my mission to gain admiration and awareness for the Wombats hockey team."

Joey thought for a moment, one finger against her bottom lip, her blond hair waving around her shoulders in a way that made me somewhat envious.

"Wait a minute," Joey said, her eyes widening. "I have a great idea!"

"Anything would be great at this point." I'd considered Declan's desire to make a movie, but lacking any kind of production knowledge or filmmaking expertise, and being a one-woman show, I didn't think that was going to be possible.

"A butt calendar!"

I stared at her. "A what? Who would want a calendar full of wombat butts?"

"Not that kind of wombat butt. Think about it, these guys—our Wombats—they have incredible physiques, right?"

"Right..." A blush tried to climb my neck, but I willed it back down. Thinking about the corded muscles on Declan's forearms, or the very prominent bulges of his biceps would serve no purpose at this moment. And I was not going to let myself think about the prince's butt.

"So, haven't you ever seen one of those firefighter calendars?"

I guessed that I had, though there weren't a lot of things

like that in Murdan. "I think so? They make those to raise money for the stations, right?"

"Exactly. It would be like that. Wombats are famous for their butts, so we can play on that and make our guys famous for their butts too," Joey said.

I wasn't sure I totally agreed with the statement that wombats were famous for their butts, since I'd literally just learned about this, but I let her go on.

"So what do you think? Can we make our Wombats famous for their butts?"

It wasn't a terrible idea, now that I gave it a little bit of thought.

"Clothed, though, right? Like, not totally naked?"

"Of course," Joey said. "We could sell them at all the games and give the whole thing an extra dose of PR magic if we used all the proceeds to help some kind of charity. And we could do a huge push on social media."

As a member of the King's Guard and someone fairly focused on security, I did not spend much time on social media. I did, however, understand that social media was probably necessary in a public relations effort.

I didn't want to reveal to Joey that I knew almost nothing about PR, but I asked her the question on my mind anyway.

"Social media… What would we do there?"

Joey assumed her thoughtful pose for a moment longer, sipping her wine and looking upward, as if all social media problems could be solved by something hanging from the ceiling of the Teakhouse Tavern. Then she said, "I've got it! Wombat wisdom."

Again, Joey delivered her idea and then waited, as if I would immediately understand the importance and genius of it. And again, I did not.

"Gonna need more."

"Well, you of all people now know that wombats are super interesting. What if each calendar image that we share on social media is accompanied by one of these awesome facts—wombat wisdom? And we could also share facts about the player whose butt is being profiled in each post."

Joey looked extremely excited about this, her eyes were glowing, and she was practically bouncing on her stool. I wasn't certain that the palace would be excited about me being responsible for revealing the prince's butt on social media alongside facts about marsupials.

When I didn't answer immediately, Joey started talking again.

"Come on, Lizzy, it's a great idea. Why don't we run it past John and Deck and see what they think?"

I wasn't opposed to running the idea past the guys, but as far as I could tell, the prince was no more of an expert at public relations than I was. He would likely be very little help, and he seemed to have a rather goofy sense of humor, which would probably mean that he'd think this was a great idea.

I was fairly certain the king would not think this was a great idea. More importantly, I did not see how taking pictures of hockey players' butts would help me convince Declan to return to his place as heir in a timely fashion.

Joey was on her phone again, furiously poking at the

screen and continuing to bounce around in her seat like whatever she was looking at was so exciting she could hardly contain herself.

"What are you doing?" I asked.

"Sorry," she said, looking up at me. "I just had an idea. And you're not gonna believe this."

I was already having trouble believing the previous conversation, let alone the fact that I had agreed to the whole butt idea. I could hardly wait to find out what this one would be.

"What is it?"

"Well, you know I work with animals, right?"

"Yes..."

"Well, I remember hearing about an exotic animal rescue nearby. It's a place where people who have illegal exotic pets surrender them, and they live out their days being taken care of and fed."

"OK..."

"Wombats are exotic."

Joey clearly thought I was following her line of thought. I was clearly not.

"And?"

"And someone in West Virginia had an illegal wombat as a pet, and they recently surrendered it to the exotic animal rescue here. Maybe the team can adopt it!"

My mind reeled. Joey wanted us to adopt a wombat? "What would we do with a wombat?"

"Do you even have to ask? It could be our mascot!" Joey's eyebrows did this little dancing thing, moving up and down toward her hairline, that told me she was even more excited than she had been about the butt calendar idea.

"A mascot?" I asked.

"A mascot is the ultimate PR move," Joey said. "Wombats are adorable, as we have already established, and having an actual wombat at games would be such a media draw."

"OK, how do we get this wombat?"

"You leave that to me," Joey said.

DECK

HOCKEY IS LIFE?

I AVOIDED CALLING MY BROTHER.

I wasn't proud of it, especially because I'd been thinking about him a lot lately. But if Lambert was calling—or rather, texting me to call him—I just had a feeling it couldn't be good news. And my selfish heart, the one that had led me to leave in the first place, abandoning my brother to his duties and to his solitude... that same heart made me afraid to pick up the phone and see what he needed. Because honestly? My life was pretty good.

Samuels and I went over the tape from the last game, and while there were a lot of contributing factors to my flawed play at the end, I did identify some areas for improvement. And that gave me some ammunition to keep in my back pocket for the discussion I knew was coming with the coach when I got to practice the next morning.

He'd scheduled a couple of one-on-ones with various players, and he'd already had the whole team rewatch certain parts of the tape, highlighting areas for improvement. My screwup was a big one.

I arrived at the rink Tuesday morning, feeling ready for my one-on-one.

"Coach?" I stood outside his office door.

Coach Merritt was bent over his desk, jabbing a pencil into a piece of paper in front of him repeatedly, as if he were giving it a good talking-to. It really seemed like the paper had probably gotten the point by now, but he gave it one more solid jab before he looked up at me and barked, "Come in."

I did, doing my best not to look scared. I was probably twice as big as Coach Merritt, but that didn't mean I wasn't afraid of what his opinion meant for my life—and my career.

"Sit down, Deck."

"Coach, hi, I—"

"How about I go first?" The coach leaned back in his chair and crossed his arms over his chest, dropping his chin a little and giving himself a couple of extra chins, which did nothing to make him look less formidable. At least, not if you were me.

"Sure, okay."

"Deck, you're part of this team's foundation."

Well, that had to be good.

"But I gotta say, son, that foundation is looking pretty fucking shaky."

Well, that was less good.

"I don't know what was going on with you in North

Carolina, but you need to know that your foundation is a little shaky too."

What did that mean? I was afraid to ask.

"I need to see nothing but commitment from you, Deck. I need to see you early to practice—no more fifteen minutes late. I need to see you be the last one here, and I don't mean because you're taking a forty-five-minute shower. I need to see you mentoring the younger guys—if you can find anyone greener than you. I need to see you listening to the vets.

"You came in here with a lot of natural talent, and that's taken you far. But to cement your spot, I need to see real commitment and dedication from you. I need to see that this isn't just a fun hobby for a guy who's got something else to do later on."

The coach finished his speech and then looked at me expectantly. I sat with his words for a minute, afraid of what might come out of my mouth if I responded too quickly. My brain ticked, working through all the possible things I could say to convince Coach Merritt how completely serious I was about the Wombats.

He didn't know my past—he only knew where I'd come from as a hockey player. He didn't know that if I didn't have this, I didn't have anything. At least, not here in the United States.

"Coach Merritt, I understand everything you're saying. And I want to assure you that my commitment is more solid than ever."

I watched the coach's gruff face as I spoke. Maybe it was just the way I felt the words pouring out of my heart, or maybe he could feel that too, because I swear the lines around his mouth and eyes softened a little.

I kept going. "There is nothing I want more than to dedicate myself entirely to the Wombats. I don't have anything else going on, Coach. This isn't a hobby for me. It's my entire life—my entire identity. And I don't want to lose it.

"I reviewed the game over and over with Samuels, and yeah, I saw it clear as day. I got too low on the forecheck and lost my guy—should've cut back sooner instead of chasing the puck behind the net. By the time I turned, their right D had all the space in the world. I hesitated, took one wrong angle, and left him wide open."

I paused for a breath, but the coach was focused entirely on me, like he was hanging on every word I was saying. I went on. "I should've pressured him, taken away the shooting lane, or at the very least, forced a pass. Instead, I gave him a clean look, and he made us pay for it. That's on me. It won't happen again."

The coach's face relaxed even more, and I thought there was a chance that the tiny quiver on the right side of his mouth might be his version of a smile. I'd seen him smile a couple of times—not very often at me. And that looked like a baby Coach smile. I was gonna tell myself that was a smile, because otherwise, I wasn't sure how to react to his lack of reaction.

"The words are right, Deck," Coach said. "Now we'll see if the action follows."

"It will, Coach. It will. All action all the time. Nothing but action. Action is my—"

"Got it."

"Yeah."

I rose and almost backed out of the room, forgetting for a moment that this was my hockey coach and not my father, the king. It was okay to turn my back on Coach, though I wanted him to know that I respected him, and if it took treating him like royalty? Then that's what I would do.

I worked hard that day—harder than I had worked in the last three years. Because I had meant what I said to the coach. This was it for me.

As I finished my long shower that afternoon, I thought about everything. I thought about hockey. I thought about home. And I thought a little too much about Lizzy.

Part of my commitment to the Wombats reinforced my commitment to Lizzy's efforts. I needed to help her. I needed to make her effort as successful as my own on the ice. Because if I could help make the Wombats a household name, then maybe Declan Gillespie would also be a household name.

And if kids had posters of me on their walls, the way we had posters of Stephano Mizzoni? The coach couldn't let me go.

I grabbed my gear, stuffed my phone in my pocket, and turned to leave the locker room.

Then my phone buzzed. I pulled it back out.

Lambert: Declan. Call me. I mean it.

A sigh escaped me, and I heard it more than felt it leave my lungs. It sounded like the sigh of a guy who was running out of ways to avoid things. I was going to have to call my brother whether I liked it or not.

I made my way across the parking lot to my truck and climbed inside.

And then I saw Lizzy.

She was sitting in her car, watching me get in. I gave her a little wave, and she gave me a nod back. Sometimes I had the feeling she was following me, or at least paying some extra special attention to me.

But maybe that was just wishful thinking.

I stared at my phone for a long moment, but staring at my phone didn't change anything. Finally, I dialed. It rang a few times before I heard scrambling on the other end of the line. A couple of seconds later, my brother's voice came through, as if from years before.

"Hello?"

"Lambert, it's Deck."

"Declan," he said, his voice clear and calm—for some reason I'd expected him to sound groggy or confused.

"How are you?" I asked, hearing myself echo the stupidest question people always asked when they knew the answer was probably not great.

"Yeah, I'm good. How are you?" How was I? Why had he pinged me twice if he was good?

"Really, Lamb? You called me because you're good?"

"I called you because you're my brother, and I miss you. Is that weird? And also—technically, I texted you. You called me."

It wasn't weird, but it was unexpected.

"Not weird, I guess. It's just that you've never, in a

decade, called me just because I'm your brother and you wanted to see how I was."

"Fair. Maybe I've matured. It's occurred to me that we are family, and we should keep in better touch."

I waited for my brother to move on to whatever the real reason he'd pinged me was, but he seemed content to have simply re-opened communications between us.

"Hey, Lamb? It's great to hear your voice and everything, but you've got me worried. It's not like you contact me all the time. And the few times you have, it's been because something was going on. I mean, I like the idea of being in touch more, but I just have this feeling there's something more to it. Is there something going on?"

"I mean... There is, but I just don't really know how much you need to get pulled into it all." Lambert wasn't doing much to put my nerves to rest.

"Lamb, I kinda feel like I'm in it now, and if you don't give me details, I'm going to think the worst. Right now, I'm imagining everything from Mom and Dad turning Murdan into a nudist colony to an army of rebel rats staging a coup."

"Rats?" He let out a small laugh. "You've always had a good imagination, Deckkie."

"Tell me," I ground out. I was losing patience.

"Yeah, okay... so, first, things are good? I mean, with hockey? With you?"

"Yeah, they're good. The season is shaping up. I had a rocky start, but I just talked to the coach and I'm recommitting. Totally, 100 percent in."

"Well, that's good. I mean—yeah, never mind. Pretend I didn't text."

My brother didn't beg me to call just so he could ask how hockey was going and then tell me to 'never mind.' And as much as I wanted to let him off the hook, I knew I wouldn't stop worrying until I understood what was really happening.

"Lambert. Now I'm worried. What's going on?"

"I don't wanna bother you... You made a choice. We've all respected your choice. But Dad is..."

Lambert trailed off, leaving me hanging on those two words: Dad is. Dad is what?

Finally, I asked him that very question.

"Look, it's nothing he's said. And Mom's not talking. But there's something going on. And I think—I mean, I don't wanna be the kid that cried coyote."

"The kid that cried coyote? Do you mean the boy who cried wolf?"

"Whatever. Yeah. I mean... Okay, I'll just say it, but you don't have to do it. I think you should come home. But I also don't wanna tell you to come home and then have you get mad because there was no reason for you to."

"Is there a reason for me to come home?" Worry—maybe even the beginning of fear—began to bubble in my gut, making me wish I hadn't eaten that meatball sub earlier.

"I don't know, Deck. Something's weird."

I wasn't sure that something being weird justified me sacrificing my hockey season and jumping on a plane back to Murdan. Especially after I'd just told my coach that this was all I cared about. The truth was, I had a couple of other things to care about, and my family was one of them.

It was just that, in the past, my family didn't need me. It had been easy enough to leave when I knew I was the spare, and my parents were healthy and vibrant.

Had something changed?

We both went silent, as if we were sitting together in the palace drawing room, sipping tea and looking out at the sprawling lawn beyond. But we weren't. And the distance between us became more solid—more real—with every second that passed in silence.

"Lamb, I've got a lot on the line here. Like, my whole career. This is a kinda make-or-break season for me. But if you say I need to come home, I'll give it all up. Family comes first."

Lambert didn't speak right away, and when he did, his voice was shaky.

"No. Don't—don't do that. I don't know why I called. Sometimes I just get in my own head."

"Lamb?"

"Yeah?"

"You're clean, right?"

He laughed. "Yeah, I'm clean."

"When's the last time you were in rehab?" I was pretty sure the one rehab facility on Murdan had a suite with my brother's name over the door, he'd been there so many times now.

"You won't like the answer."

"Just tell me."

"Couple months back."

"Lamb..."

"Look, the two things are unrelated."

I rolled my eyes. "Being clean and rehab are not related?"

"Listen, this is not why I called. And now I'm actually sorry I did. I shouldn't have bothered you. You left, and that is what matters. We should all just respect the distance and leave you to hockey."

The words were right, but the delivery left a stone sinking in my guts.

"You called to tell me something about Dad."

"Yeah, but just pretend I didn't. Good luck this season." Lambert hung up.

I stared at my phone, and a text came through from Lambert.

> Lambert: I'm sorry. Forget I called.
> Everything is fine.

It was pretty clear that everything was not fine.

I put my phone down and stared out the window for a long moment, feeling like reality had shifted somehow. Moments ago, my life had been 100 percent about hockey and the Wombats. Now, an unwanted second priority was edging in—one I'd put away a long time ago.

Did my family need me?

CHAPTER 18

LIZZY

FAMILY-FRIENDLY SUGGESTIVENESS

I SLEPT on the ideas of the calendar and the wombat, but I didn't wake up with anything more exciting. So when I met with Declan after practice the next day, I was ready to tell him about both.

"Lizzy," he said. "How's the movie coming?"

That's right—he still thought we were making a documentary.

"Well, I think the plan has changed." I walked toward a couple of the arena seats and we sat down without either of us suggesting it.

"Well, if you come up with something better, I think that's great." He was smiling his usual wide smile, but there was something in his eyes that worried me. He didn't look excited about the idea I was about to tell him—or, really, about anything.

"Declan, is everything okay?"

Something shifted across his face, but I couldn't read it. I only knew there was something on his mind—something he wasn't telling me.

"Yeah," Declan said. "It's great." He smiled even wider then, but the smile was as false as the jewels in the tiara the Queen wore when she traveled outside the palace. "Tell me your idea, Lizzy."

"Well, it's about butts."

Declan's smile dropped from his face, then reappeared —more genuine than before. He started laughing, and I realized I didn't have the same charisma Joey did when she'd first come up with the idea. It didn't sound the same coming from me at all. It was going to be difficult to sell this idea.

"Did you say the new idea is about butts?" Declan could barely get the words out, he was laughing so hard.

"No—I mean, yes, I did say that, but it isn't what I meant." I gathered myself, straightening my shoulders, tensing my spine. I was a woman who could single-handedly take down three guys in a hand-to-hand fight. Why was I having a hard time explaining the idea of a calendar? "Let me try again."

"I think that's a good idea," Declan said, still smiling.

"I'm thinking we should do a calendar," I said, speaking slowly and trying to start with the basics.

"A calendar?" His face was unreadable. I couldn't tell if he thought this was a great idea or a terrible one.

"Right, but it would be like a 'Wombat of the Month' kind of thing—like the ones they do at fire stations."

"Fire stations?" Declan did not seem familiar with the concept of the of-the-month calendar.

"Right, so sometimes, I guess, firefighters pose in somewhat provocative ways for calendars. Then they sell those calendars to raise money for charitable causes. Or maybe just for the firehouse? I don't really know."

"Provocative, you say?" He was grinning now.

"Right. So for the Wombats, we would focus on… well, on your butts."

Declan burst out laughing again, and I knew I still hadn't done this great idea justice. I started explaining—loudly, talking over his laughter—until I finally got the full extent of Joey's idea out.

"And by the way, this was Joey's idea," I added, just in case Declan thought it was a fantastic idea, but also in case he thought it was the worst one he'd ever heard.

"Got it. And would we also be raising money for a charitable cause?"

"Oh yes, I forgot that part. And that's maybe even the best part."

"Yes, charity is a good idea."

"Right, so—we're going to adopt a wombat."

The look on Declan's face told me I had failed again at selling this idea. His smile was bright, his eyes were dancing, and if nothing else, I had at least distracted him from whatever had been bothering him when we first sat down.

"Lizzy, I don't want to burst your bubble, but I don't think adopting a wombat is something you can just stroll into PetSmart and do."

I knew that. Why didn't I start with that?

"Right, no, I know. But there's a wombat at an exotic animal rescue in West Virginia. Or Virginia. Or somewhere.

And Joey works with animals, right? So she talked to them, and they've agreed to let us adopt Wilma the Wombat as the team mascot."

"Wilma the Wombat. I love it." And I loved the way he was looking at me. It gave me confidence to continue, and made me feel warm all over.

I went on to explain to Declan the connection between the wombat and the whole butt thing, which I still hadn't really managed to convey properly. But once I got it all out, he understood—and thought the whole thing was amazing.

"Lizzy, this is brilliant. Pure genius. This is PR gold."

I wasn't sure if Declan was qualified to judge whether PR ideas were gold or genius, but I didn't really care. For some reason, his approval—his excitement—mattered more to me than actually accomplishing my goal.

The way he was grinning at me gave me tingles that reminded me so much of the feelings I had as a little girl, playing with this same boy in the palace. The boy who made everything fun, made everything feel possible.

"Let's talk more about this calendar," Declan said, one side of his mouth lifting in a way that made me want to trace the expression with my finger, maybe detour a bit to feel the scruff of his jaw. It looked soft, and I had a sudden urge to rub my fingers through it. Which I knew was not a normal thing for a PR consultant to be feeling about the subject of her public relations.

Unless you were, unfortunately, attracted to someone you were not supposed to be attracted to. And if you acted on that attraction, I thought, public relations suddenly became private relations. And that was not what I was here for.

"What would you like to know about the calendar?" I asked.

"So you say it will feature our butts," Declan said slowly. "Are we going to have to be, um… Are we going to have to be naked for this calendar?"

"No!" I felt the blush climb my cheeks, and this time I couldn't stop it. Declan saw it too—I knew, because his eyes tracked it up my cheeks, all the way to my forehead. Then those blue eyes tracked back down my face, landed somewhere around my mouth, and hung there for one torturous second. Finally Declan's eyes returned to mine.

"Is it going to be… suggestive?" He asked, putting undue emphasis on that word.

"I mean, suggestive, yes. But in a way that is family-friendly," I assured him.

"Not sure you understand the meaning of the word suggestive," he said.

I did. I thought everything about Declan was suggestive. But I couldn't tell him that.

And maybe I did need to do a little more research on what kind of suggestivity was appropriate for a calendar kids would see at Wombats games.

"Lizzy, I'm proud of you. These are fantastic ideas. And having a wombat as our team mascot? An actual live wombat at the games? That's gonna get so much coverage. Plus, I think it's gonna make kids really happy. And making kids happy is awesome."

Declan's face was open and bright, and it made me feel happy too. But then a little shadow creased his brow.

"Actually… I don't really know much about wombats. They're not, like, vicious, right?" His voice was heavy with concern.

"I don't think so," I told him. "Unless you get too close to their butts, I guess. But that would only be if you were trying to get into their burrow, I think. It might warrant a bit more research before we introduce Wilma to children."

Declan nodded, and for a moment, we sat in silence, side by side. I shifted my gaze, staring out over the ice, where Declan and the other Wombats could do things on skates that I didn't think most people could do on dry land.

There was the stiff scent of ice in the air, and this close to the dugout—or the bench, or whatever they called it—there was an undertone of something completely masculine. I also caught a whiff of Declan's clean scent.

He must've taken a quicker shower today, I thought.

All of it combined to make me wonder a bit—about how I had found myself here, in this place, with this man, who was like an old friend but also a new and very interesting acquaintance.

After a moment, Declan turned to me. "Walk you out to your car, Lizzy?"

Little did he know, I was actually going to walk him to his car.

But it didn't hurt to let him believe he was protecting me.

"Sure."

CHAPTER 19
DECK

SUCCESS AND CELEBRATION.
IDIOT.

THE FOLLOWING WEEK WAS A WHIRLWIND. My mind was torn in so many directions, I fully expected to play like shit. I kept thinking about the call with my brother —he'd sort of insinuated that my dad might not be doing well. Or that something was going on with Mom? At any rate, I knew things at home might not be good. But had I given up my right to be worried about them?

If that was true, why had Lambert called?

And just the knowledge that he was still using was plaguing me. I knew I should tell my parents, but I had a feeling they already knew.

We were on the road again, this time facing the Land Sharks in Toronto. I was determined to be 100 percent focused on travel and practice, going into the game at the Land Sharks' arena.

Lizzy was with us, which was a bit of a distraction. But she kept her distance, and I often saw her wandering around the perimeter of the arena, as if she was trying to get her steps in or something. She was a very interesting woman, and the more I got to know her, the more I wanted to date her for real.

But Lizzy had made it clear, in no uncertain terms, that there was nothing between us.

The thing was, I wasn't sure I believed her.

At this point? I didn't want her to fake date me. I wanted her to real date me.

But I also didn't need the coach on my back about the no-fraternization rule.

Miraculously, very little of that was on my mind when I took the ice against the Land Sharks. It felt a lot like like redemption. The Land Sharks came in hard, throwing their weight around early, but we didn't let them dictate the game. We matched their pace, played smart, and every line showed up ready to battle. It wasn't perfect—no game ever is—but we stuck to the plan, controlled the neutral zone, and forced them into mistakes. The energy on the bench was different tonight, like everyone knew we had this one in us. And when the final horn sounded, the scoreboard backed it up.

For me, this felt like the game I needed. After that mess last time, I knew I had to be better, and I was. I stayed sharp and made plays instead of watching them happen. Set up our first goal with a clean cross-ice feed, then buried one myself in the second—picked the top corner off a rebound, and didn't overthink it. Even off the puck, I was where I needed to be, cutting off passing lanes, winning board battles, making the kind of plays that don't show up on the scoresheet but make the difference between winning and losing.

Walking off the ice, sweat still dripping, all I could think was: this is how it's supposed to feel. Not frustration, not regret—just that deep, buzzing satisfaction of knowing I did my job. We did our job. The Wombats took care of business, and I made damn sure I was part of it.

The Land Sharks played at our arena two days later, and the games were like bookends, cementing my confidence that no matter what was going on at home, this was where I belonged.

On my way out of the arena that evening after our home game, I bumped into Coach. He did something he rarely did—he stopped me by the arm, spun me to face him, clapped me on the back. And he smiled the whole time.

The next day, we had a team meeting before an easy practice and then a day off. Lizzy was there, looking nervous.

"Hey," I said, smiling at her. I was happy to see her. I was always happy to see her.

"Hey," she returned. "I'm supposed to tell the team about the PR idea today."

Ha. That's why Lizzy looked so nervous.

"Well, it's a great idea, and you know it. And I've got your back."

"Thanks, Declan. I might need it."

I shook my head. "You won't. You'll do great."

A couple of minutes later, the coach urged us all to sit. And by urged, I mean yelled until we did it. Then, with very little by way of introduction, he pointed at Lizzy and gestured toward the front of the room.

To her credit, she marched up there like she owned the place. I marveled again at her confident posture—and at her biceps.

Since she'd been here, I hadn't had a chance to ask about her lifting regimen, but I guessed she'd been keeping it up. And the dresses she wore did nothing but favors for her physique.

Not that I should have been noticing any of that. But I couldn't help it.

"Hi." Lizzy blushed in the front of the room, and my chest constricted a tiny bit.

I wanted to rush up there and help her. I didn't want her to feel uncomfortable or nervous. This was just us—the dudes, the guys, the Wombats.

But I understood why she might have felt a little pressure.

"So, as you know, I have been brought in to build, reinforce, and amplify the image of the Wilcox Wombats." Lizzy was about to continue, but she couldn't—because there was loud cheering, hooting, and clapping from the team.

She smiled, waiting for them to calm down, and I could see the applause had given her a bit of confidence.

I was glad.

"Anyway, I brainstormed with both Declan and Joey Baxter, and I think I've got a couple of really great ideas for you. But I don't want to do anything without the team's full approval."

Lizzy paused, clasping her hands in front of her and

looking around the room. Her shoulders were back, her chin was high, and I could see that confidence returning.

"What's the plan, then?" Coach asked in a gruff voice.

"Well, it's really threefold. The first part is linking the team to a charitable cause. Combining forces with another organization amplifies any public relations efforts we make. And any kind of time or money we can give to a charitable organization only benefits the Wombats—by demonstrating your commitment to the community in which you live and work."

Well done, Lizzy.

The Wombats clapped and cheered again, until the coach gave us all dirty looks and told us to shut up.

"So that's part one—we need to select a charity that fits the bill.

"Part two will sound a little strange, but please bear with me. I'd like to spend some time doing a photo shoot with the Wombats team members."

"A photo shoot?" The coach did not sound excited. "These guys aren't models, Lizzy. Some of them don't even have all their teeth."

After he said this, Adam Wyler popped up and removed the bridge that held the four front teeth he'd lost last year when we played against the Storm Chasers. He held the bridge up like a trophy, grinning his gap-toothed smile as everyone laughed.

Lizzy, however, looked a bit concerned.

"Don't worry, I'll keep them in for the pictures," Adam said before taking his seat again.

The room quieted, and Lizzy continued. "The idea

would be to put together a charity calendar featuring the Wombats and highlighting one particularly impressive feature of real wombats."

I waited for the delivery of the final bit, hoping Lizzy could do it—hoping she'd practiced a bit more than when she'd told me the idea.

"I don't know how many of you are familiar with how wombats behave in the wild, but they are fascinating creatures. They're marsupials, which you probably know, but their pouches are actually upside down," she said, looking around at the gathered men who all wore slightly quizzical expressions. "That's so that when they dig, which they're really adept at, they don't end up shoveling dirt into the pouch."

"Ah," murmured a few more interested players.

"And even though they're pretty short and squat, they move astonishingly fast, like twenty-five miles an hour."

"Just like Van!" yelled someone in the back.

"Shut it," Van said, sounding amused.

"They also do an interesting thing with their feces," Lizzy said.

But Sly Remington was already talking. "Yeah, yeah. They poop cubes. And they stack them, like Jenga towers. It's amazing."

"Leave it to Sly to know everything there is to know about wombat poop," Rock Stevens said, earning a laugh.

"Right, but the other really amazing thing about these creatures is the way they use their butts." The laughter had already begun.

Coach stood up and faced the room. "Is there ever going

to be a day when any of you might not act like six-year-olds?" The answer was no. But nobody was going to say that to the coach. We quieted down and waited for Lizzy to finish.

"So when a predator follows a wombat into its burrow, trying to eat it, the wombat squats down low and waits until the predator's head is above its rear end. Then, with amazing force and power, it pushes its body up against the burrow entrance and crushes the predator's head between the hard, plate-like structures of its butt and the top of the hole."

"Killer butt," Solamentes said, looking pleased. There were other sounds of glee around the room, and when it was quiet again, Lizzy went on.

"So, the calendar would highlight this aspect of your anatomy as well—but in a tasteful way, of course. We could sell the calendars at the games, and all or some of the proceeds could benefit the charity you select."

Everyone looked at the coach expectantly.

"Yeah, fine. Good."

Lizzy looked as surprised as I was that Coach had bought in. That was great. She still needed to talk about Wilma the Wombat, but Coach was already diving into his expectations for the next week, when the team had a bye. He pointed at Lizzy, telling her this would be the best time for the photo shoot. She agreed. We were excused then, and Derek Reed approached Lizzy at the same time I did.

"Hey, Lizzy?"

"Yes?" She turned to him.

"I think the calendar's a great idea. And I have a friend

who's a professional photographer. I don't know her schedule, but I could ask about next week if you haven't already lined one up?"

"That would be amazing. Thank you."

I stepped closer to Lizzy's side, my arm brushing against her elbow. Her skin was soft, and I could feel the slight tremble in her body. "Killed it, Lizzy."

"Thank you," she said, smiling and relaxing a bit. "I honestly think telling you first was good practice for presenting it to the coach."

"Well, he bought in. Success and celebration." I had no idea why I said that. It didn't make any sense. I felt like an idiot.

But Lizzy made me nervous sometimes.

CHAPTER 20

LIZZY
DEEZ NUTZ

THE NEXT WEEK, the Wombats had a bye, which was perfect because Derek's photographer friend Janice had an opening. I met her at the arena in the morning, just as the guys were finishing practice on the ice. She set up some lights and a backdrop, though we ultimately decided it wasn't necessary. The Wombats' arena itself was a perfectly good background, but we kept the backdrop set up just in case.

"You know, I normally spend my days photographing children," Janice told me as we set up. "So this is going to be a nice change of pace."

I tried to imagine what a job photographing children might be like, and all I could picture was pure chaos. Once, I had orchestrated a picnic on the green in front of the palace for all the nearby children. To put it lightly, it was a shitshow. Toddlers running everywhere, screaming, literally pooping their pants. I mean, I know that goes hand in hand with having kids, but I just don't think that's something I could handle. At least not right away. Then again, I guess once you go through all the trouble of having a kid, you're pretty aware that this comes with it.

But I digress.

"Yeah, although the Wombats often do act like children," I pointed out.

"Yes, maybe," Janice said. "But at least these children are hot."

She had a point.

Rock Stevens was the first of the Wombats to be photographed, and the man had no compunction whatsoever about exposing his rear end. The idea was to have the players pose in various states of undress—wearing their hockey gear and sort of not wearing it at the same time. Rock skated out onto the ice, carrying all his gear and wearing only boxer briefs with a huge squirrel on the front and the words "Deez Nutz" pointing at the center.

I felt my face heat, and I didn't even bother trying to stop it. But Janice? Janice was a special shade of scarlet I wasn't sure I'd ever seen before.

"Rock," I said, my voice coming out higher than I intended.

Rock stood before us, flexing and posing without any direction whatsoever.

"Yes?" he asked.

"I thought we'd start with all your hockey gear on, and then maybe take off a few select items as we progress."

I had thought this through a little, and at least with Declan's photos, I wanted to stay somewhere between G and PG-rated. Rock, on the other hand, was clearly prepared to go somewhere between R and X.

Rock's face fell. It seemed we had crushed one of his dreams—one that apparently involved appearing nude in a calendar.

"Sure, yeah, whatever." He skated back off the ice, took off his skates, and started putting on his full gear.

A few minutes later, Janice and I had both regained our usual skin tones, and Rock reappeared—fully clothed this time.

Janice took over. "That's great, okay. Can you hold your stick—"

"Oh, I hold my stick plenty," Rock grinned.

"Rock, that's enough." Wow. I had just channeled a kindergarten teacher. I didn't know I had it in me.

"Yeah, sorry, Lizzy." Rock looked ashamed—as he should.

The rest of Rock's session went just fine. He was happy when we finally asked him to take off his jersey and pads and pose looking over his right shoulder, his hockey gear still on display.

It took several hours to get through the Wombats' lineup. And because there were more than twelve players, we were obviously going to have more than twelve pictures —something I hadn't really considered. I didn't want to be the one picking and choosing who made it into the final twelve months. I made a note to talk to Joey about it. Of course, it was possible some of the pictures would be unus- able—like the one where Freddy Elks insisted on bending down, looking between his legs while standing on his skates, and sticking his tongue out. Not very sexy.

Declan was the last to shoot.

He skated onto the ice, looking taller and broader than usual, thanks to the skates and pads. And for a second, he took my breath away.

Literally.

The prince was so handsome, I often forgot what kind of effect he had on me. And if I didn't steel myself properly before seeing him, there were usually a few seconds where I found it difficult to think, breathe, or speak.

"Lizzy, are you okay?" Declan had spoken to me. I hadn't noticed, because I was overwhelmed.

"Yeah, sorry."

"So, how do you want me?"

Oh, the ways I could answer that question.

But no. This was my job. Part of my job. At least, this was my fake job. And I was going to take it seriously. Declan was not asking me how I wanted him in general.

"I'll defer to Janice. She's the expert."

"I'm an expert at taking shots of kids with bunny ears in front of Easter balloon arches," Janice whispered behind her hand.

We'd been battling Janice's impostor syndrome all afternoon. It didn't help that she found every single Wombats player attractive—even Garrett Ackerman, who was literally missing two of his bottom front teeth.

In the end, Declan was a natural. Maybe it was all those royal family portraits he'd sat for as a kid, but he seemed to instinctively understand what the camera wanted. When

Janice suggested he strip down to his boxer briefs and come back out with just his jersey and skates, I thought I might have a heart attack.

The boxer briefs did nothing to hide the fact that the royal jewels were more plentiful than I had imagined. Declan, for his part, was not shy. He wasn't Rock Stevens in terms of exhibitionism, but he wasn't embarrassed either. He turned and posed, waving the package around until I was struggling to breathe.

"I think that's enough," Janice said. I could have kissed her in gratitude.

Declan looked at me then, and it was hard to hold his gaze, knowing that he was standing there nearly naked from the waist down. It was also hard to not let my gaze skitter lower.

But I think I managed admirably.

"Lizzy, will you wait for me? I'm gonna get changed."

It surprised me that Declan hadn't figured out by now that I always waited for him—or that I followed him home to make sure no one else followed him home.

"Yeah, of course." I ignored the raised eyebrows Janice was shooting my way, but as soon as Declan disappeared toward the locker room, she had questions.

"So… you and the winger. Are you a thing?"

"No," I told her. "We're just… we're friends."

"Sure," she said. "You seem very interested in your friend."

The blush was back. "No, no, I'm not. I hope I didn't give him that impression."

"You wouldn't be alone," she said. "'Cause I'm pretty sure he's only got eyes for you too."

I didn't know how to respond to that, so I didn't.

Later, when Declan found me outside, he hesitated, like he was nervous about something. "There's a party tonight over at Klaus's house," he said. "I wondered if you might wanna come with me?"

I wanted to scream yes. I wanted to run to him, throw my arms around his neck, wrap my legs around his waist, and show him yes. But I settled for, "Yes."

Declan grinned, looking slightly surprised. "Yeah?"

"Yes. That sounds fun."

"Look at you, ready to have fun," he teased.

I rolled my eyes. "I'll go, but what will the team think this time about us showing up together?"

Declan's smile faded just a little. "Lizzy, I'd like to take you as my date. My real date."

I swallowed hard. Was dating Declan what was best for us? I could argue that getting close to him romantically would serve my mission.

But that wouldn't be my real reason.

DECK
MATCHING DOGS

"OKAY," Lizzy said with a smile, and something inside me released.

She'd said yes!

"You're sure?" The second the words were out I wanted to smack myself. I did not want her to change her mind.

"If you are," she said, her smile turning shy.

"I'm sure," I told her. "I'll handle the guys."

She nodded, and together, we went out to my truck. Lizzy tried to argue that she was going to drive, but I reminded her that this was a date. I was driving.

We headed to the gated community where Arndt lived and pulled up to his insane house. It was three or four stories if you counted the basement, which he'd turned into a hockey rink. The party would certainly be out back, where he'd had a heated pool, a hot tub, and a massive patio and outdoor bar and kitchen installed. We used to hang out at Mizzoni's, but once he moved out to Los Angeles, it seemed like Klaus Arndt was more than happy to fill the void. As I helped Lizzy out of the truck, I could hear the music blasting.

"We just go in?" she asked as I reached for the front door handle.

"No one will answer if we ring the bell," I explained, letting myself into the house as I'd done hundreds of times before.

"He might want to think a bit more about security," she said as I pulled the door open. "Holy…"

Lizzy looked around the house. Arndt was very into white, so all the furniture was white, and the light gray hardwood was scattered with white rugs. He had two enormous white Afghan hounds, who greeted us as we stepped into the sunken living room.

"The dogs match."

"They do," I agreed. "This is Ryan and Blake."

Lizzy frowned at me. "He named his dogs after…"

"His favorite celebrity couple, yes."

"Weird."

The dogs followed us to the patio doors and we headed outside to where most of the team lounged around the pool or hung out at the bar. When they spotted me with Lizzy, it was as if the music stopped and everyone froze. Of course, that isn't what happened, but I could feel the questions.

"Let's get a drink," I suggested, guiding her to the bar. We took two stools next to Derek Reed, one of our centers, who grinned as if he'd just thought of the funniest thing in the world.

Julius Ramon sat at the end of the bar, chatting with

Chris Houstein, and he lifted a hand and sent a smile as we got settled.

Derek was staring. "You're the PR chick," he told Lizzy as she scooted in next to him.

"And this is Derek. Master of the obvious," I told her.

"Yeah, sorry. I'm Derek." The idiot looked at me over Lizzy's head, his eyebrows shooting up.

"I know Derek," she said.

I didn't have time to answer because Arndt was there next, moving behind the bar to stand in front of us. "Hello Deck. Hello date of Deck."

"You know Lizzy," I reminded him.

"Nope, I don't. Because Lizzy works for the team, so you couldn't be dating her without breaking some rules," he pointed out. "So this must be someone else. We'll call her… Tizzy."

"That's insane," Lizzy said.

"But not against the rules," Arndt quipped. "What can I get you, Tiz?"

Lizzy sighed and asked for a scotch, neat. A couple of the guys whistled their appreciation for her order.

"Deck?" My teammate asked.

"He likes pink wine," Lizzy said quickly, eliciting a laugh from the guys who were eavesdropping.

"I'll take a beer," I suggested. "It's a little early for pink wine."

Arndt produced a beer for me and then gave me a meaningful look, shaking his head.

It was true, dating Lizzy could get me in trouble. But I found that compared to the warm certainty I felt when I thought about her, I wasn't too worried about the rest. Besides, I was on Coach's good side now.

For the most part, the team was well behaved, asking questions about her work and thanking her for what she was doing, trying to get the team a little more exposure. The other women at the party were welcoming too, and at one point, Lizzy went to play ping pong with a group of ladies across the patio.

"You're playing with fire, huh?" Panther Aspen pulled up a chair next to me. "Is it worth the burn?" His words were laced with suggestion, and they made me want to sock him in the mouth.

"None of your business, you know?" I sipped my beer.

"Coach know about this?"

"No, and he doesn't need to," I suggested.

"Hard secret to keep, man." He was right, but I wasn't going to waste time worrying.

"I'm just trying to help her get a decent story here," I told him. "Get close enough to us to really capture the spirit of the team in her PR efforts."

"So you fucking her is a public service?"

"No, that's not what I meant…" I shook my head, unwilling to engage in whatever little game Panther was trying to pull me into. It was a relief when John Samuels slid into the seat on my other side.

"Hey, how's it going?" His warm smile always did something to ease whatever tensions I'd been feeling. John was a truly good guy.

"Things are good," I told him. "Just a little bit of crazy going on at home, and a lot of pressure this season here."

He nodded. "I get the pressure. You know, you don't talk about home much."

I met his eyes. Sometimes over the past couple years, I'd wanted to tell somebody the truth. Especially John. I just had a feeling he'd understand, that he might even have some good advice for me. But I couldn't do that. "Yeah, my childhood was... different."

"Different how?"

Shit. Why didn't I just blow this off? "Like... I was just carrying a lot of expectations as a kid. Family stuff. And then I ended up getting raised by an uncle kind of far away from my parents."

John's smile dropped. "That sounds rough, Deck."

"No, that was actually the good part."

"Oh shit. I"m sorry, dude. And you still talk to your parents?"

I realized I'd just implied something totally different from the truth. But maybe that was for the best. "Yeah, they're good people. I talk to them now and then. We just ended up going really different directions."

John nodded, staring down into his beer bottle almost sadly.

I was about to say something else, but I paused as Lizzy approached. "Hey you." I wrapped my arms around her waist and pulled her close, nuzzling her neck. It was supposed to be just a quick gesture, just a taste.

Only my body didn't get the memo, and things inside me went haywire. She smelled like heaven, and every nerve inside me was suddenly on overtime.

Lizzy tensed in my grip and then relaxed against me, and I nearly lost it.

"Hey," she said, pulling back. "I was just gonna ask for the car keys. I left my bag in there and I want to grab my lip gloss."

"Oh, yeah, I can grab it for you." I hopped down off the stool and headed for the glass doors.

"I can get my own bag out of the car," she argued, following me.

"I've got it. I'm being gentlemanly," I said as we crossed the living room.

"You're being condescending. If we are dating, you need to know that I'm a very independent person," she argued as we stepped out the front door.

"I'm a very caring guy," I explained, pulling the keys from my pocket and pointing them at the truck.

"I can get it myself," she said, grabbing for the keys as I swiped them out of her grasp. I held the keys over my head and Lizzy jumped up and down, trying to wrestle them from my hand. "Give them to me!"

"You're not being very nice," I told her.

"You. Are. Not. Being. A. Gentleman." Each of her words was punctuated by a vertical leap. She was getting good height on each one, but with my arm straight over my head, she didn't have a chance. "Give me the keys, Declan!" There was something about seeing her exasperated, all flushed and gritty, that I just couldn't resist.

"Why don't you make me?" I don't know what came over me, it wasn't like me to stand in the front yard refusing to help a woman, but Lizzy had managed to twist this whole situation around until I was suddenly not helping her at all, I was basically keeping her from getting what she wanted.

"You want me to make you give me those keys?" she asked, stepping back and crossing her arms.

A little thrill went through me. "I'd like to see you try."

Two seconds later, I was flat on my back, Lizzy sitting on my chest and the keys in her hand. "How the hell…?"

"Now you know," she said, annoyingly proud of herself. She continued to sit on me while she aimed the fob at the car again and pressed unlock.

But this time, the car didn't merely chirp and unlock.

It.

Exploded.

CHAPTER 22
LIZZY

PIECES OF TRUCK

I THREW my body over the prince as his truck exploded into flames, sending a huge cloud of smoke and debris up into the street and making a horrific noise.

Players came streaming out of the house and through the gates from the back yard, and neighbors were stepping from their houses to watch the burning remains of Declan's truck at the curb like some kind of neighborhood cookout.

"Holy shit, dude, did you miss a recall notice?" Rock Stevens asked Declan, stepping closer.

I lifted myself from his body, ignoring the fear zooming through me. That had been far too close. I needed to get the prince home. Immediately.

The fear I felt was more than just the worry appropriate for someone who'd almost lost their target in a protection assignment, though. It was more in line with the kind of fear a person felt when someone they cared about was in real danger.

And I did care about Declan. Too much. Which was why

this assignment had been a bad idea in the first place. Even if no one else remembered it, we had history. And that was interfering with my ability to do my job objectively.

"I guess I must've," Declan said, picking himself up off the grass and brushing off his shorts as the big car smoldered and sirens sounded from some distance away.

"Why is your vehicle burning in front of my house?" Klaus Arndt asked, sounding irritated as he looked up and down the street at the pieces of truck scattered about.

"Sorry for the inconvenience," Declan said, rolling his eyes.

It was hours before we were able to leave. First the fire department came, and then, when the explosion was tracked to a bomb strapped beneath the truck's chassis and set to ignite when the doors unlocked, we chatted with the police investigators for a while longer.

I could have told them everything I knew, but it would blow my cover. I had strict instructions from the royals, but I wondered if this might change things. If Declan knew his father was sick… if he knew how unstable things were as a result, how much danger he was in as long as he remained here in America…

I knew I wasn't supposed to tell him, but I didn't see any other way. How would I convince him to go home otherwise?

I had one idea, but if it didn't work, I resolved to tell the truth, even if it meant potentially losing my job. His life was too important.

"I'd like to offer you a ride home," Declan said as we sat in the office where we'd been waiting at least a half hour at the police station for them to let us know we could leave. It was well after midnight, and the prince looked as tired as I felt.

"That's okay," I told him. "I'm sure the police will give us a ride."

"I haven't been driven home in a cop car since I was sixteen," he said, chuckling. "But hey, I'm a pretty exciting date, huh?"

I leaned into his side, both for the warmth and reassurance, and because I was exhausted. But once I was there, I found very little resolve to move back to where I'd been before.

Declan's big arm came around me, and for a long moment, I just breathed him in. He smelled like grass and fresh air, and a lingering hint of smoke.

The police did give us a ride home, and as we sat together in the back of the cruiser, Declan's arm was around me again.

"Who would do this?" He asked in a low voice. "Who would try to hurt a hockey player?"

But I knew that somewhere deep inside, he knew it was about more than that. If he told me the truth first, then I could tell him everything. I wasn't glad our lives had been threatened, but it might have opened the door to accomplishing my mission.

"You really have no ideas?" I asked, trying to sound like I didn't either.

He sighed, and the sound carried the exhaustion that I was sure came with keeping secrets. Keeping big secrets for years. About your identity, about your past… about your future.

"Why don't you come to my place?" he suggested. "I worry about you being alone after this…"

I looked up into his blue eyes. "Come home with me instead," I suggested.

It was clear the prince took that as more than the simple invitation I'd hoped it would be, as his eyes darkened slightly and he swallowed hard. I'd suggested it because I knew the security at my place was tight. I'd coordinated all the details myself from Murdan, and confirmed that everything had been done exactly as I'd specified upon arrival. There were no other tenants in the building, and the doormen were on the royal payroll. There was no safer place to be in Wilcox, Virginia.

CHAPTER 23

DECK

THE COUCH WANTS IN

I WANTED to go home with Lizzy. But not for the obvious reasons. I wanted to go home with her so I could tell her…something. Could I tell her everything? Did I maybe have to now?

"Yeah," I said, tightening my grip on her shoulder. "Yeah, I will."

The cop drove us back to her car, which was parked at the rink, "Thanks," I told him as he pulled up in front of her sedan, and I slid out and then turned to give Lizzy my hand.

"Any time," the cop said. "And we'll follow up with whatever intel we get on who might have been responsible."

"Sounds good," I said, suddenly exhausted. Despite my fatigue, however, I knew there was a long night ahead. And not the fun kind of long night. Although, the way Lizzy had been looking at me since the explosion—like she'd really be sad to see me get hurt—maybe there was a chance.

Lizzy drove us to her place, and I thought the whole quiet drive there. Hockey players didn't get their cars blown up. But you know who did? Princes. Royalty. But only if there was a reason for it. And as far as I knew, there wasn't one.

We greeted Arnold of the signed gut and proceeded to the eighth floor, where Lizzy lived.

"Pretty snazzy," I commented, looking around the sleek and modern condo. Really though, it was kind of sad. Everything was perfect. Clean. Uncluttered. There wasn't a single item on a shelf that indicated who lived here. No photos, no knick-knacks that didn't look like things the model home designer chose. "You lived here long?"

"No, not really," she said. Lizzy stood in the center of the living room, looking around as if she'd never been here before either. "I guess it's a little…unfinished."

"It's nice though," I said, not wanting to be rude.

Lizzy blew out a rough breath and then moved into the kitchen, just beyond a long black counter. "I don't have any pink wine. Hope Scotch will be okay."

"Yeah, that sounds good."

She carried two tumblers over and put the bottle on the low coffee table, then sat on the long white leather couch. I took a seat next to her.

"I need to tell you—"

"There's something I should—"

We spoke at once.

"Ah, you first."

"No, you go first," she said. "I insist."

Gah. Should I tell her? Could I really? Would it blow

everything I'd worked for over the last decade or more? But at this point, it felt like my cover had been literally blown when my car had exploded.

I swallowed most of my drink, then turned to look into Lizzy's wide eyes. "The thing is… I'm not quite who everyone thinks I am."

She just stared, waiting.

"So, I mean, like, I am. But I'm more than that."

She nodded, and then Lizzy's eyes found mine, and there was so much warmth and acceptance in them that it stopped me in my tracks. I wondered if that would all disappear once I told her I'd been lying to her this whole time.

I hadn't felt this way about anyone in a long time—maybe ever.

Like she was my equal. Like she was my second half. Like she was the puzzle piece I didn't even know I'd been missing.

But I needed to tell her the truth. It seemed like it was literally life or death at this point. And if there had been an attempt on my life, what did that mean for Mom and Dad? For Lambert? For the entire kingdom?

I'd had a good run. I guessed my time was up. "Thing is, I just… I need to tell you who I really am."

I took a breath, ready to tell her everything, but Lizzy interrupted. "Declan, I know exactly who you are." Between the look in her eyes and the way her gaze drifted from mine to my lips and back up again, her own mouth parting slightly, I couldn't stop what happened next.

I closed the space between us, pausing just long enough

to give her time to pull away if that was what she wanted. But Lizzy didn't hesitate. Our mouths crashed together, and within moments, we were a tangle of arms, moans, and heavy breaths that ratcheted my desire for her beyond anything I'd thought possible.

We fused together on the length of Lizzy's pristine white leather couch. Every time I shifted my weight, the stiff leather gave an obnoxious squeak. As things escalated between us, the couch seemed to participate—hell, it even seemed to accelerate its efforts.

I managed to remove my shirt, and Lizzy's hands explored every inch of my torso, her gasps and moans sending a thrill through me as my own hands mapped the curves I'd been desperate to touch since the first time I saw her. The couch groaned beneath us, the squeaks turning into something closer to protests.

"Lizzy, do you have a bed?"

"Yes, Declan. I have a bed." Her words were spoken between pants, our hands never stopping.

"Could we go there?" The couch let out another long squeak as I shifted my knee.

Lizzy didn't answer with words. Instead, she practically lifted me off the couch, nearly carrying me down the hall to the open doorway beyond, where an enormous bed waited.

"Lie down," I suggested.

But Lizzy, it turned out, was not the compliant type. "Take off your pants," she said.

I, for one, didn't mind being ordered around. Especially in this context. I complied. "Okay, but what about your pants?"

A wicked smile crossed Lizzy's lips, and some instinct took over—I kissed it. I kissed the smile I'd been wanting to kiss since the first day I saw her.

And kissing Lizzy? It was everything I thought it would be. And more. Kissing Lizzy was like every day being your birthday, topped off with cotton candy, ice cream, all the scotch you could drink, and zero regrets.

I wanted Lizzy more than I had ever wanted anything. It occurred to me that I liked her as much as I liked hockey. And that was saying something.

Lizzy refused to lie down. Instead, she spun me and then climbed me, pushing me back onto the massive mattress, which, by the way, seemed even bigger than my own California king.

I came up for air, glancing around. "California king?" I stretched my arms, testing my wingspan to see if it reached both sides. "I mean, it's really big."

Lizzy sat up and gave me a look that made me realize discussing the size of the bed was probably not what we should be doing at this moment. But she humored me anyway, because Lizzy liked me. "It's an Alaskan king, if you must know."

I raised a brow. "But you're a tiny person." Lizzy did not appear to enjoy being called tiny. I swear she started flexing some of the muscles in her chest and arms, because suddenly, she looked far more intimidating straddling my naked body than she had a moment before.

"Those are fighting words," Lizzy growled. Then she attacked again. The woman was everywhere. And I was in heaven.

As a hockey player, I'd had my fair share of meaningless hookups. Women always seemed to enjoy the mystique of pro athletes. I didn't really understand it, but as long as it worked to my advantage, I wasn't going to argue. Lizzy, however, didn't seem the least bit fazed by my status.

In fact, she seemed hell-bent on subduing me. Dominating me. Teaching me a lesson.

I was here for all of it.

CHAPTER 24

LIZZY

FAKE SURPRISES ARE NO FUN.

I KNEW Declan had been about to tell me the truth. And it wasn't that I didn't want him to tell me the truth—honestly, that was my whole mission. That, and getting him home. The problem was, I wanted to steal just a couple more minutes of being Lizzy, the PR consultant. Because as the PR consultant, my responsibilities were neatly contained within the limited scope of the job I was pretending to do. I wasn't responsible for a kingdom or the sanctity of the throne. More importantly—or really, more selfishly—I knew there was a chance Declan would hate me when I revealed my deception.

I didn't think about any of that as his hands skimmed over my body, leaving trails of fire in their wake. My own breathing, my own moans, surprised me. I wasn't even sure if they were actually mine or if they belonged to Lizzy, the PR consultant. Because I'd been playing a role. And there was something gratifying and sexy about maintaining it—

getting to be a whole other woman. A whole other kind of woman in Declan's arms.

Lizzy the operative intimidated men. She was one of them—strong, capable, maybe even a little masculine. She wasn't this wanton, sexy girl in a hockey player's bed. Okay, well, technically it was my bed, but you get the point. So who could blame me for wanting just a few more minutes to be that girl?

And Declan?

He was everything I could never have dreamed he would be when I was nine years old. He was caring, he was gentle, but there was a fire inside him that stoked my own. And as our mouths and bodies clashed together in a manic, tension-filled push and pull, I felt something shift. Not just between the two of us, but cosmically. It was as if, with every thrust, every grasp of his hands, every move of his hips, Declan was realigning reality.

For me, at least.

I'd begun the encounter wanting to dominate, but once my guard had slipped, thanks to Declan's persistent thumb rubbing a firm circle against my clit and making me lose my patience and some of my self control, I let him flip me onto my back. And then, almost infuriatingly, he backed off. He was straddling me, but then he rolled to one side and sat up on his elbow, smiling down at me.

"Why are you stopping?" I panted. I'd been very close to reaching that point where my brain stopped its constant anxious churn. I needed him to keep going.

"I wanted to look at you for a second." His eyes scraped across my skin, taking in my breasts, my heaving chest, my quivering stomach, and everything below. I wasn't the least bit embarrassed, because I was looking at him too.

"Like what you see?" I asked him, though it was obvious from the way his engorged cock throbbed against my hip that he did.

He let out a low growl, and then he was rolling onto me again, taking my earlobe between his teeth and biting gently. A thrill shot from there straight to my core, and my hand wrapped itself around his cock.

"I think it's time to see what you can do with your stick."

He pulled back. "Was that a hockey joke?"

I rolled my head back and forth against the pillow. "I'm deadly serious."

He grinned, and his eyes hooded as I stroked him, hard. "Hang on, I have a condom," he moaned, rolling off me again to search for his wallet. When he finally came back, packet in hand, I felt like I might explode.

"Let me." I snatched the packet from his hand and rolled the condom down his length. "Now go."

"So demanding," he chided, but he didn't waste any time lining himself up. I grasped his back with my hands, trying to pull him into me, but Declan controlled the motion, sliding into my wetness slowly. Slowly enough to force me to arch upward to get what I needed. Contact. Friction. Fullness. I wanted it all.

Just as he was nearly inside all the way, he pulled back, and the whine that escaped me surprised even me.

"So impatient," he whispered, finally pressing all the way in. I felt my eyes roll back in my head, and the breath leave me—it was perfect. It was everything. And finally, finally, my brain quieted and I was only sensation.

He pumped slowly, and I was powerless beneath him, enjoying every second more than the last. Every muscle inside my body felt like it was gripping as tightly as it possibly could, and just as I struggled for control, my brain introduced a thought that sent me right over the edge: *You're fucking the prince…*

And as we ascended to the very precipice of some mountain I hadn't even known existed, I wanted—more than anything—for this to be real. But as I lay in his arms afterward, both of us sticky with sweat and satisfaction, I knew a conversation loomed ahead that would change everything.

"I'm gonna have to get an Alaskan king-size bed, I guess," Declan said.

"Oh, you think that was the bed?"

Declan grinned at me, those blue eyes dancing. I couldn't help but lift my hand to rub it along the scruff on his jaw, which was every bit as soft as I'd imagined.

"There's only one way to find out," he said, mischief thick in his voice, making it deep and throaty. "We'll have to do it again somewhere else. Maybe the kitchen counter?"

God, I wanted that. But I needed to talk to him.

"Maybe we should talk instead?" My voice was uncertain, because everything in my body was uncertain at that moment—a sensation I didn't like and was not accustomed to.

"Yeah." Declan did not look like talking was his first choice either, but I saw the same resignation in his face that

I felt. There were things to discuss. "I bet you're wondering why my truck blew up today."

I smiled at him. I wondered if I knew more than he did about why his truck had blown up, but I didn't say that.

"Yeah," I said, hoping he would continue.

"Well, I probably should've been honest with you before we… did… this." Declan waved his hand between us, as if the incredible sex we'd just had was a physical presence in the room. Honestly, it almost was.

"That's okay. Just tell me now."

"Well, there's some stuff about me that you don't know. Stuff about my past."

Any other girl might have told him that we all had skeletons in our closets and not to worry about it. But I knew what he was about to say wasn't just a skeleton in his closet—it was much deeper than that. It had to do with his very identity, and I needed him to tell me.

"Would you believe me if I told you I'm actually a prince?" Declan looked sheepish now, as if this was the most far-fetched thing he could possibly say.

I took my cues from him, but second-guessed myself the moment I faked surprise. At what point was I supposed to come clean? The broad strokes were outlined in my mission, but the details, the subtleties of maintaining a trusting relationship with this man while confessing that I'd been lying to him—that hadn't been made clear.

"A prince," I said slowly, working to keep my expression blank. "A prince of what kingdom?"

"It's a tiny island nation that most people in the US

haven't heard of. It's called Murdan," he said, watching my reaction.

I said nothing, my brain working furiously to decide how to handle this. When did I tell him who I was?

He sat up, something colder settling across his face. "Lizzy? Why don't you look surprised?"

I swallowed hard. "I don't know what to say," I admitted. It was the most honest thing I'd said to him since we'd met.

"This is not exactly the reaction I was expecting. Is it that you think I'm crazy? Do you not believe me?"

I sat up and turned to face him, pulling the sheets up against my naked body, doing my best to prepare myself for whatever was coming next. "Declan, I haven't been altogether honest with you, either. The reason I'm not surprised is because I already knew who you were."

"That's impossible."

I tilted my head, not liking the hurt I saw on his face as he began to grasp the reality of my lie. There was nothing to do at this point except reveal everything.

"I know, for instance, that you are second in line to the Murdan throne. I know that your older brother, Lambert, has been struggling and may not be the best fit to take over for your father, Erik. I also know—and you may not—that your father is unwell. And while this is a closely guarded secret, anti-monarchist rebels have found out, and they see it as an opportunity."

Declan's face grew more and more stern with every word I spoke. My heart twisted inside my chest until I could barely breathe.

"And how exactly do you know all of this?" Declan physically moved away from me, across the massive mattress, until he was standing, pulling his clothes off the floor and shoving his feet into his shorts. "It's a little convenient, isn't it, that since I've met you, there have been guys coming for me? My truck blowing up? Lizzy, are you part of the anti-monarchist rebel group trying to overthrow my father?"

I might have smiled. I didn't mean to, but it was so absurd. I'd given my entire life to the protection of the crown. The idea that I would do anything to harm it… "No, Declan. Absolutely not."

"I don't suppose there's any way for you to prove it, though, is there?" He pulled his shirt on over his head.

"There is, actually." Abandoning any modesty I'd felt before, I dropped the sheet, rose from the bed, and strode across the room, opening the top dresser drawer and removing a long case. Inside were my palace ID badge and my Commendation of Valor.

I opened the box in front of Declan, holding it out to him like an offering, and stared at him as he took in the information before him.

CHAPTER 25
DECK

THIS EXPLAINS THE GUNS…

LIZZY HELD OUT A THIN BOX, the kind you'd keep jewelry in. She flipped it open to reveal a commendation bearing my country's crest. The other item inside was an identification card that looked just like the ones worn by my father's personal guard. With her photo on it.

"What is…" I shook my head.

I couldn't figure out how I felt—so I defaulted to the most easily accessible emotion. Anger. "You knew? This whole time, you knew?"

I thought about all the time we had spent together, about the way I'd tried to help her—felt sorry for her, even—and all the while, she'd been lying to me. The entire time. And what an idiot she must think I was, knowing full well that I was actually the Prince of Murdan, playing hockey guy over here in the US.

It was humiliating. It was infuriating. I had no idea what else it was. I just knew I didn't like it.

I sat down on the edge of the bed, staring at the woman

who was no longer just the PR consultant with the kickass body—the one I had just had sex with—but who was, in fact, a member of my father's guard.

Sent here to…

That was a good question, actually. Why was she even here?

"Is your name even Lizzy?" I asked, feeling like everything was up for grabs at this point.

"I go by Lizzy now."

"Now?" I stared at her, that odd sense of familiarity tightening around my ribs. That feeling I'd had since we met.

If she went by Lizzy now…

I asked the question. "What did you go by before Lizzy?"

"When I was young, I went by Eliza." Her voice softened as she said it, and something flickered in her eyes. Seeking what? Understanding, maybe.

I was in no place to give her understanding. I was furious.

But at the same time, I suddenly knew exactly who she was. "Eliza? Eliza, as in the girl I played with when I was young? You grew up in the palace? Your mother is—"

She cut me off. "But I can explain everything—"

"You lied to me. Not just about who you were, but about why you were here." I let out a short, humorless laugh. "Or are you actually a PR consultant in addition to being part of my father's elite guard?"

Lizzy tilted her head, looking both ashamed and slightly

amused—if that was even possible. "Did I strike you in any way like a professional PR consultant?"

I thought about that. She definitely had no idea what she was doing in the PR department. "Maybe I should've seen it."

I stared at her, her face almost rearranging itself into the features of the girl I had once known. The girl I had once— Then another thought hit me.

"Why are you here, Lizzy?" My voice came out harder than I intended. "Why are you here pretending to be a PR consultant?"

"I'm on a mission." Lizzy stood there in front of me, completely naked—which, under normal circumstances, would have been extremely distracting. But with everything else going on, her nudity was only slightly distracting.

"And that mission is…?"

"Don't you know?"

"At this point, can't you just tell me?"

Lizzy sighed, and the sound carried so much exhaustion, so much hurt, that I almost wanted to console her.

But I held on to the one feeling I was sure was real. Anger. "Was your mission to come here and seduce me?"

I wasn't sure why that would make sense—how would it help my father to send one of his guards to seduce me? It didn't matter. It was possible.

"No, that wasn't it." She met my eyes. "I was sent here to bring you home. Your father is ill. Gravely ill. And Lambert might be next in line, but he's not seen as a stable candidate. And as long as that is true, the kingdom is in a precarious position. There's a coup underway, but you're the linchpin."

"What do you mean?" None of this made sense… did it? The call I'd had with my brother came back to me suddenly.

"As long as a legitimate—and stable—heir exists, there's a strong sentiment in the country for secession. But with you gone and your brother… a bit unreliable…"

"There's a plot to overthrow my father?"

"Declan. I don't know how to tell you this," she said, her face falling. "Your father probably won't be around much longer…"

I dropped my head into my hands. "I knew something was wrong." Fear and sadness welled inside me as I thought about my father being ill, possibly dying. I'd left so easily, never looking back. But that had been because my father… well, he was the fucking king. He was invincible. He'd been young and healthy when I left. But now?

Lizzy moved closer to me, the sympathy and understanding on her face almost believable. "I'm so sorry."

"I don't understand why he didn't just tell me."

"Because you have to return of your own free will in order to take the throne, and you have to be in the country for your brother to abdicate. They needed you to choose it."

"How could I choose it if I didn't even know this was going on?" I shook my head and stood again. I couldn't make this make sense. "I don't understand."

"I know. I'm sorry." Lizzy took another step closer. "But I'm relieved to be able to finally discuss it with you."

I scanned her face as another thought occurred to me. "You volunteered to bring me back?"

"Not exactly."

"You didn't want this mission."

"No. I mean, no offense, but chasing down a hockey-obsessed prince isn't quite the same as taking out a dictator with a long-range rifle inside the perimeter of an enemy country."

"You've done that?" I wasn't sure whether to be impressed or concerned for my safety.

She shrugged. "What'd you think the commendation was for?"

I stared at her for a long moment, my understanding of the woman in front of me—the girl I'd once loved—rearranging itself into something new. I didn't even think the words before they were escaping my lips. "Don't get me wrong, I'm still pissed. But Lizzy?"

"Yeah?" Something in her expression made my breath come faster, my voice deepen.

"You're the sexiest woman I've ever met."

One heartbeat later, she reached for me and slammed into my arms, our mouths meeting and tiny explosions erupting everywhere inside my body.

CHAPTER 26
LIZZY

GOING COMMANDO.

MY EMOTIONS WERE a tornado inside me. I threw myself at Declan, relief at his acceptance and fear at his rejection twirling together into some torment of emotion that could only be expressed physically. Luckily, he seemed to be on the same page. And I didn't blame him.

My hands found the hem of his shirt and pushed it off his muscled torso as if my life depended on it. The second his skin was bared. I dropped to my knees, kissing a trail down his chest to his navel, and then immediately helping him out of his shorts.

I barely had a moment to think before he had me off the ground in his arms and was carrying me through the apartment. He made good on his promise to try out the kitchen counter, and despite the frigid chill of the stone beneath my butt, that was hardly the first thing on my mind.

Declan laid me across the countertop and I didn't have a second to breathe before his mouth was on me, one hand teased one breast while his mouth laved and sucked the nipple of the other. Everything inside me responded and I gasped and arched beneath him.

It was as if conscious thought was on some different plane than the one which we inhabited in those moments. My body reacted, my breath, my voice, my hands, all directed by some primal instinct brought to life by Declan's insistent ministrations. Then, he raised up, fitting himself to my entrance, and he shocked me by grinding out in a gruff, angry voice, "Get ready, Lizzy. Take me in."

Something about the anger laced in his words, the ferocity with which he thrust into me, and my own feral desire for him had me meeting each move of his hips with my own aggression.

I could barely breathe, the sensations ratcheting through me were so intense. I had a momentary fear that I might actually die. But it would be worth it, I thought.

Declan's calloused hands circled my hips, pinning me to the kitchen island as he penetrated me deeply over and over again, my body responding to each thrust, despite my mounting exhaustion. Even if I didn't want to climax, Declan was going to force it from me, and the sheer virility of the prince fucking me against the kitchen island was a thought so lascivious it nearly finished me. I knew I would be thinking of it later and it would be all I would need to reach the same point, even if I were alone.

I heard myself scream my release at the same moment as Declan's voice rose in something that sounded like an animalistic roar. His hands never left my hips, and as he slumped across my body, both of us heaving, his hands slid higher, crossing beneath my back until he was holding me to him tightly. And what had begun as a fierce sexual battle concluded in an intimate tender hug.

"What do we do now?" he asked softly.

"I need to get you home, Your Highness."

Declan held me like that for a long, long time, and I knew his mind was racing through all the implications of leaving Virginia so suddenly.

My departure wouldn't be without complications either. I had grown fond of my position with the Wombats, and wanted to see it through. But that would be impossible.

"How quickly can you pack?" I asked him.

"Do you think it's even safe to go back to my place?"

That was a valid question. And one I thought I should have thought of. "You stay here and I'll go. Tell me what you need and where I can find it."

Declan released me and stepped away, his expression serious as he gazed into my eyes. "No, Lizzy, it might not be safe for you either."

We had both forgotten who I really was. A hazard of the job, I supposed. But now I needed to regain my former identity.

I slid off the island, stable on my feet once again, and looked into the prince's eyes. "This is exactly what I'm trained for, Declan. I will go get what you need, I will be back in an hour. And then we will go."

"It just doesn't feel right."

"What doesn't? Leaving suddenly, or me doing my job? "

"All of it. Any of it."

I knew it would take a while for the prince to come to

terms with his duties, and with the fact that his father was not well. But my mission was clear and I would complete it.

I dressed quickly, forgoing the PR consultant wardrobe I'd been wearing since I'd met Declan here in the United States. I pulled on a functional pair of black pants and a tight fitting long sleeve black shirt that concealed my weapon. And as soon as I got everything together, I left.

CHAPTER 27

DECK

SACRIFICING THE SAUCE.

AS SOON AS Lizzy was out the door, I began texting her a list of things I would need.

I had no idea how long we would be gone. I guessed maybe forever. But I couldn't take everything I owned, even if everything I owned reminded me of the freedom and wonder of a life lived away from being royalty.

> Declan: 12 pairs of boxer briefs. Please get the bright pink pair. It's my favorite for workouts.
>
> Five T-shirts. Be sure to get the one with the panda breaking a chair over the other panda's head and the one that says "pew pew" in the Star Wars font.
>
> There's a bunch of jeans in my closet. I hate most of them, so pick the ones you think you like best. Can princes wear jeans?

I really had no idea what proper attire for a prince in his

home kingdom might be. I hadn't played that role in a long time, and none of the clothes I'd worn when I was ten would fit me now.

The list got longer and longer as I thought of things I would miss. When I got to Chick-fil-A sauce, Lizzy stopped me.

Lizzy: Declan, we should not take perishable goods.

Right. No Chick-fil-A sauce. Dammit. We didn't have Chik-fil-A in Murdan, though.

Declan: You sure no sauce?

Lizzy: No Sauce.

I waited, wondering what Lizzy would encounter at my house. Would there be armed assassins waiting for me? Would she be okay? And after I thought about that, I wondered how Lizzy even knew where my house was, since she had never been there with me.

But then again, Lizzy wasn't Lizzy. She was Eliza—an elite member of my father's guard. Eliza had killed people, I guessed. Did that change the way I felt about Lizzy?

The whole thing was super confusing. I didn't know how I was supposed to feel about anything at this point. The only thing I was sure of was that I was worried about my dad. And about Lambert, if I was telling the truth. I wanted to call him, but I also didn't want to tie up my phone in case Lizzy needed me.

Then again, would Lizzy really need me? Would a

woman capable of the things Lizzy was capable of ever need a man? The woman I had come to know had never made me feel inferior in any way. Well, maybe that one time when she flipped me onto my back on Arndt's lawn. But honestly? That was kind of hot.

Still, Lizzy might've been more man than I was.

For a lot of guys, their masculinity might have felt challenged. But I poked around at mine, and either it wasn't as sensitive as some dudes' or it just wasn't very well developed, because it didn't feel challenged at all.

More concerning was the lie. I understood why Lizzy had to lie. But that didn't mean I had to like it. And it left a whole lot of questions in places where growing certainty between two people becoming intimate really belonged. Without that certainty, how did I know if we were compatible? How did I know who this woman really was?

We'd been close when we were nine. What did that mean now? I sighed deeply, leaning back into Lizzy's very squeaky white couch. The squeaks and groans of the couch seemed sympathetic with my own groans of despair.

The only thing that was certain was that I was going home.

Not to visit.

Not to check in.

But possibly, to rule.

Lizzy was back not an hour later. She came upstairs, telling me she had packed three suitcases for me. If I couldn't fit what I needed in three suitcases, I probably didn't need it.

"Are you ready, Your Highness?"

I stared at Lizzy. I wanted her to be Lizzy, the PR lady. I didn't want her to be Eliza, the terrifying operative. I was kinda hot for them both, but that really wasn't the point right now.

"Hey, can we quit with the Your Highness stuff?" It was the least I could hope for.

Lizzy stared into my eyes for a long beat, and I could see uncertainty working through her dark gaze. It wouldn't be appropriate now that I knew she knew who I was. But I didn't care. "Is that what you really want, Your Highness?"

"For God's sake, yes."

"OK. Are you ready to go?"

"Would it matter if I said no?"

"Kind of. You're supposed to come of your own free will. If that wasn't the case, I would've knocked you out and hauled you onto the plane the first day we met."

"Very reassuring."

Lizzy gave me a half-smile and shrugged, and I found myself willing to go. Because she was going with me. That didn't change the confusion I felt, but at least I wasn't alone.

As we moved toward the door, my gaze slid frantically around Lizzy's impersonal apartment. "Isn't there something you should take? Like… like this candlestick?" I held up a tall brass candlestick that had been sitting on the long table behind the couch.

It was nothing personal—I knew that—but it seemed like in order for Lizzy to have been a real person, a person who I'd become involved with, she needed to have some kind of attachment to this place. Maybe to this candlestick. Hopefully to me.

"The only thing I really need is coming with me," Lizzy said, her eyes softening.

"I hope you don't mean your gun."

She laced her fingers through mine then, and my erratic heartbeat calmed a little. "Come on, Declan. We need to get to the plane."

Lizzy drove this time.

She spent a whole lot of time looking in the rearview mirror, which made me think we were being followed. She told me it was just standard practice when it was possible we might be followed. I did not want to be followed. I did not want any more men attacking me in parking lots. Or following me through 7-Eleven. Or blowing up my truck.

And I wondered—if I accepted the rulership of my kingdom, would that sort of thing be my day-to-day? I didn't remember trucks blowing up being a common part of royal duty, but I'd been pretty young.

We arrived at a private airfield an hour later. It shouldn't have surprised me to see a jet with my family crest on the fuselage waiting for us.

Lizzy parked on the tarmac, having been waved through the security gates when she showed her ID. It became clear she had called ahead. The guards waved us in, and once my door opened, they were at my side, escorting me to the jet.

I felt like… royalty. And I didn't like it.

Lizzy took a few more moments to join me, helping the men on the tarmac load my bags into the aircraft. Then she made her way up the stairs, and the door was sealed behind her.

"We're really doing this, I guess," I said, telling myself more than her. None of it seemed real. I was just a hockey player. I had a game next week.

"Shit," I said. "I need to call Coach."

"There's Wi-Fi on the plane," Lizzy said. "You can call him now."

"What do I tell him?"

Lizzy thought about that for a moment, pulling her bottom lip between her teeth and gazing out the window. "I think you can tell him the truth."

"I doubt he'll believe me."

"Well, in the grand scheme of things, it doesn't really matter."

I stared at her. Of course, it mattered. It was my reputation. My career. Everything. And I was just supposed to walk away, letting Coach believe I'd said I was committed and then simply changed my mind?

I turned away from Lizzy, walked down the aisle, and took the last seat on the left side of the plane. I strapped myself in and pulled my phone from my pocket. I inhaled deeply and called Coach.

"Declan," his gruff voice came through the line immediately. "Is this about your truck exploding? What the hell happened?"

"It's kind of about that, yeah." I tried to figure out what I was supposed to tell him. How could I explain any of this?

"Are you okay, son?"

Shit. The last time I'd seen Coach, he smiled at me. And now he was calling me son? I had finally found the place on the team I was looking for. He finally trusted me—was beginning to rely on me even.

And I was running away. Because I had to.

"Kind of. Not really," I said, hesitating. "The thing is, Coach, I'm gonna have to go away for a little while."

"Deck, it's the middle of the season." He didn't have to say anything more. Any committed player knew that leaving in the middle of the season wasn't an option.

"I know, and I'm so sorry. My dad... my—" My voice actually cracked as I tried to say the words, as I tried to tell Coach the only truth I thought he'd understand. "My dad is really sick. I don't think he's gonna make it. I haven't seen him in five years, and I need to go home."

Coach was silent, and I imagined he was working through all the things he might say. For a man who leaned toward gruff and unapproachable, he'd already shown me that he had a sympathetic and rational side. And that's what he brought out now.

"I understand, son. You take the time you need. The Wombats will be—what the hell?" I didn't know what was happening. One second, Coach sounded like he was going to be okay with me taking some time, and the next, he was screaming into the phone.

I heard a string of profanities laced with words I would

never have put together myself, but which I filed away for creative cursing later. Every third word was Wombat, and I began to wonder if maybe Lizzy's mascot had finally arrived.

"This thing is an ankle biter!" There was some shuffling and grunting on the other end of the line, then a door slammed. A moment later, Coach came back on. "We have a mascot now, Deck. Did you know that? They're calling her Wilma. But she's a freaking terrorist. The thing keeps getting loose, and it's been trying to burrow into the carpet in my office. Whenever I try to stop it, it bites my ankles."

So Wilma had arrived. I was bummed I wasn't going to get to see her.

"That's not good." I was trying really hard not to laugh. I didn't think laughing at his predicament would make Coach more sympathetic to my situation.

"It's not." Coach took a few deep breaths, and I waited. Then he said, "Look, Deck, I have to get going here. This place is a fucking zoo, and I'm not saying that figuratively. You take the time you need, and just get back here as soon as you can. But family first, son. Always."

The line went dead.

So I hadn't told him the truth. I hadn't told him the whole truth, but I had told him as much as I could. Some part of me was certain I'd be back. Because I couldn't fathom giving it all up when I had worked so hard for everything I had.

Still, I knew who I was. I knew what I'd been born into. And even though I had outrun those expectations for more than a decade, they had finally caught up with me. I shoved my phone back into my pocket just as the plane taxied for takeoff.

Lizzy didn't get up and join me in the back of the plane, and I didn't move to sit with her. I needed some time.

I needed time to understand my feelings about her. About her lie. About why she lied. About my own future. Nothing was what I had thought it was, and to say I was feeling disillusioned would be a massive understatement.

Once we were airborne, I reclined my seat and closed my eyes. Soon, we would be in Murdan.

And I would be the prince again.

And possibly the heir.

CHAPTER 28
LIZZY

WILMA IS A DUDE.

AS WE BEGAN the journey back to Murdan, I felt a shift between Declan and me. I was no longer just Lizzy, the PR girl, and he was no longer Deck, the hockey player. Suddenly, he was my sovereign prince once again, and I couldn't disregard the many layers of society that stood between his place and mine. True, I had lived and worked in the palace my whole life, but that did not make me royalty.

Aside from the structure of society itself lodging between us like a wall, I felt a coolness from Declan that I hadn't before, and I knew it was anger. He felt betrayed, confused, hurt—that I had been operating in his country's best interest without his knowledge.

My own loyalties were confusing. I wanted him to trust me. I wanted more than that from him, if I was honest. But hadn't I betrayed his trust through my very loyalty to our country? I didn't see any way around the paradox. I could not be loyal to both my king and to Deck Gillespie, the hockey player. And so, whatever lay between Declan and me—whatever intimacy, whatever... relationship?—was at an end.

My heart felt heavy as I pulled my phone from my pocket. The best thing about private jets was that you could use your phone throughout the flight, as long as you had signal or Wi-Fi. And I still did. I dialed.

"Hey, Lizzy," Joey answered after the first ring.

"Hi, Joey. How is everything?"

"Yeah, good. Busy at work. Also, the wombat is giving me a run for my money."

"What do you mean?"

"Well, the shelter did allow me to adopt him, but he doesn't seem excited to stay at work. So I've been bringing him home with me at night."

I tried to imagine bringing a wild animal into my house. I'd seen some videos online of wombats in domestic situations—would it be like having a cat?

"Oh. I thought the wombat was a girl?"

"I thought so too, when we called him Wilma. But he's a boy."

"Oh. Okay. Well, I'm sort of calling to check in on all of that." How did I tell her that she had adopted a wombat for a mission that no longer existed? "The thing is, I've been reassigned."

"What does that even mean? You sound like you're a secret agent or something. Ha."

If only she knew. "Yeah, no, it was kind of an emergency mission. Or—I mean, assignment. My firm needed me to fly to the Caribbean to oversee a new resort launch. And I'm gonna be here for a while."

"Well, that doesn't sound terrible."

"It's good, but I am having to kind of step away from the Wombats."

"Oh. Does Deck know yet? He's gonna be so bummed. You two were really hitting it off."

"Yeah. I told him. But the thing is, I wondered if there's any way you might be able to oversee finishing that calendar? And I don't even know what to do about the wombat."

"Well, don't worry about Wilma. I've already been familiarizing him with the arena. I don't think the coach likes him a whole lot. But this weekend will be the first game where he officially appears.

"The calendar though… how much is left to do?"

Joey sounded hesitant to take on the calendar project, and I didn't blame her. She had her own job.

I was about to let her off the hook when she said, "I bet the guys will finish the calendar if I kind of help them with it."

"The guys? The hockey players?"

"Yeah, the Wombats were really into this whole idea. They all have different skill sets. I bet they can cobble this thing together. Oh, by the way, they chose a charity I wanted to run by you."

"Oh, that's great. What did they pick?" In all the excitement, I'd forgotten about the charity piece.

"There's an after-school sports and daycare program in Wilcox that needs new equipment and funds for other stuff.

The guys want to donate to that, and a few of them have volunteered to run a hockey clinic at the arena."

"That's perfect!" It really was. I loved anything that would benefit the local community—especially the youth.

"John already works with them, so he's talked to the executive director and they're really excited about the partnership."

"Oh my gosh, Joey, you're seriously the best. And you don't mind kind of managing the guys through the rest of the calendar process? We just need to choose which photo is on which month, pick some wombat facts for each month and get someone to lay it out and print. Oh, and post the social stuff." Guilt threatened to swamp me. I was pushing off responsibilities onto someone else—something I would never do in my real job.

"I don't mind at all. It benefits me too—or at least it benefits John, and that helps me. When he's happy, I'm happy."

"Thank you, Joey. I owe you." I really did, and I didn't think there'd ever be a way to pay her back.

"Well, maybe you can get us a trip to that fancy resort you're working on."

"Resort?"

"The assignment you're on now?"

Oh, yes. The lie. "Oh, right. I'll definitely see if I can do that."

"Okay, Lizzy. Have fun. Don't worry about anything here."

"You're literally the best, Joey. Thank you." I ended the call, guilt adding to what already felt like heartbreak inside me. My body was heavy, and I wondered if I'd even be able to get out of the plane seat when we landed. Everything felt like it was pushing me down, turning my muscles and tissues to concrete.

I had one more call to make. I lifted my phone again and dialed the palace.

"We've just heard from the pilot. We understand you're on your way." News traveled fast in small countries.

"Yes, Your Highness. We are en route now."

"Well done, Eliza. Once again, you have served your country well." I did not feel like I had served anyone well. Everything inside me was a disaster, but I had completed my mission. And until this point, that was what my life had been about. Why did I suddenly feel like it wasn't enough?

"Mom?" The prince's voice came from behind me.

"Declan, you should really be sitting with your seat belt fastened," I told him.

"Oh, sorry, are you pretending to be a flight attendant now?" Declan's voice was laced with contempt, and I didn't blame him.

"Declan, honey," the queen sounded relieved to hear Declan's voice.

"Mom, you could've just told me. I would've come."

"Son?" Oh, yes. The royal conference call. Neither of Their Majesties seemed able to take a phone call alone. I wondered what the queen would do if King Erik really did die. She would have to answer the phone by herself. I immediately felt guilty for the thought.

"Dad, hi." Declan sounded relieved and worried to hear his father's voice. He sank into the seat across the aisle from me, leaning toward the phone I held in my hand. "How are you doing, Dad?"

"I'm fine, son. Happy to hear you're on your way home."

"Declan, you know we couldn't just ask you to come," Her Majesty said. "We had to do it this way. Don't blame Eliza."

I appreciated her suggestion, but I doubted it would do much good. Even I blamed Eliza.

"What's going on with Lambert?" Declan asked.

"There will be time to explain everything when your feet are on Murdan soil, son." The king sounded weary but optimistic.

"We should land in about four hours," I said, checking my watch.

"We will see you soon, then," Her Majesty said.

I ended the call and looked up at Declan. He met my eyes but did not offer a word. And through the beard on his face and the inscrutable blue of his eyes, I had no idea what he might be thinking. But I was pretty sure he wasn't thrilled with me.

Declan slept the rest of the way home. Or at least he kept his eyes shut and didn't speak to me.

I watched the endless sapphire and emerald sea beneath the wings of the plane, undulating endlessly, unaffected by the turmoil of our tiny human lives. That sea had always calmed me as a child, and I remembered watching it from the Murdan beaches, the prince at my side. It had always made me feel small, but in a good way. I took comfort from it now as it grew nearer and nearer to the landing plane.

When we touched down, Declan stirred at my side. The plane jolted, and he grabbed for my hand across the aisle, surprising me—and clearly surprising himself. "I had a dream we were crashing," he said, letting my hand go as if it had burned him.

I tucked my fingers into my lap and gave him a smile, doing my best to disguise the pain I felt at the distance between us now.

It had been a fun adventure, but clearly, my time as Lizzy the PR rep was over.

CHAPTER 29

DECK

IN WHICH WE REFERENCE
SWAFFLING.

THE HEAT of Murdan hit me like a ton of bricks. It was like being swaffled in the face with Derek Reed's just-removed practice pants. Unpleasant, to say the least. (And unfortunately, I speak from experience.)

Add to that the obsequious guy bowing to me on the tarmac, and I remembered immediately why I didn't come home more often. I did not want to be a prince. I did not want to be royalty. I did not want to be here.

All the same, I slid into the back of the sleek limousine my father had sent for me. I had a duty, whether I liked it or not. And that duty did not involve pads, pucks, or flying across the ice like I had no cares in the world other than pounding the opposing team's center into the boards.

It was a short ride to the palace. It was a short ride everywhere in Murdan; the island nation was only a hundred square miles in total. Palm trees swayed on either side of the car, and the low cottages that made up most of the island's neighborhoods spread out around us, punctuated here and there by colorful shops and even more color-fully dressed people. Murdan had a casual vibe, which I appreciated. But as soon as you stepped into the palace, the difference was clear. We had once been a British colony, and the royals still upheld many of the traditions handed to us by our colonizing forefathers.

The car pulled to a stop inside the palace gates. I wondered if Lizzy would be joining us. Eliza, I meant. I didn't want to miss her. I didn't want to think about her. But, of course, I did.

It wasn't her fault I was here. It wasn't her fault that I had left when we were children and that she'd gone on to live her life in service of the crown. I couldn't be mad that she had built a life for herself. It wasn't my place to say what choices were right or wrong for her.

As angry as I was—about how things had turned out, about how she had deceived me into this outcome—I didn't blame her. Not really. In fact, I probably owed her an apology.

"Your Highness." The man who had greeted me at the airfield pulled the door open and then waved for me to step out. I did, spotting my mother and father standing on the steps to the palace.

The building behind them, which we called the palace, did not look like Cinderella's castle at Disneyland. It was the royal estate, but it was more sprawling resort than towering castle. There were no spires or turrets to be found —just miles and miles of long, low terracotta buildings, filled with treasures and luxuries befitting a king.

It was a place where, as a kid, there had been many

rooms off-limits to me. A place filled with endless twisting hallways, where it was easy to lose oneself in a game of hide and seek.

"My son." The king stepped gingerly down the stairs toward me, his arms wide open. I stepped into them, wishing I hadn't noticed how thin his limbs felt as they encircled me. My mother was just behind him, a tear rolling down her face as she joined our hug.

Even though we were monarchs, even though our lives were lived in duty to our kingdom, we were still a family. And I loved them more than anything else.

Despite all the complications, it was good to be home.

After a few moments, my mother stepped back, and my father took my arm, walking me up the steps and into the palace.

Everything was just as it had been five years earlier, when I last visited—understated opulence at every turn, the occasional unexplained vase on a pedestal, or a helmet displayed inside a lighted glass cabinet in the hallway. I had never understood this detritus of royals gone by. It all seemed a bit cinematic to me. Maybe that was part of why I'd had to leave.

I was not cut out for royal life.

"There's much for us to discuss," the king said, still holding my arm and walking like a man with many years ahead of him. Not a frail leader, about to abdicate the throne.

We entered the royal residence, which was a house within the house—the place I had grown up, where my parents had raised Lambert and me.

"Where is Lambert?" I asked, looking around, as if he might materialize from the parlor or step out of the hallway leading to the bedroom wing.

"I expect he's at his own apartment," my mother said. "Lowell, could you—?"

The man who had discreetly followed us inside nodded and left, off to find my brother.

We sat on the casual couches surrounding the low table in our living room. My mother sat close to my father on the couch across from me, taking his hand and resting her head on his shoulder. I sighed, taking them in.

They both looked older, I thought. Less resilient. I didn't want to see it. I wanted to think of them always as the healthy, sturdy people who had raised me. But that was the inevitable turn of the world, wasn't it? People aged. Parents died.

"Why am I here?"

Mom's face immediately fell, and I knew my words had hurt her.

"I mean, I'm here because I love you, and I understand that things aren't good. But why the urgency? What's changed?"

"I have cancer, son," my dad said, delivering the news I had known was coming.

"What kind?" I asked. I didn't want it to be true. I didn't want any of this to be true.

"Lymphoma."

I looked between my mother and father, who were gazing at each other tenderly. "How long have you known?"

"They detected it a month ago," my mom said. "We're waiting on some test results. We'll know more soon." She delivered this as if it was good news, but it didn't change the truth of it. My father was dying.

My father looked as if he had long ago accepted this news—the impending arrival of his death. I was having more difficulty with it.

"Dad..."

"We're all gonna go sometime, son. Now my job is just to make sure that I take care of the people I love—and those I'm sworn to protect. And that's why you're here."

I shook my head. I had known this was coming—kind of. But it was still hard to take in. It was hard to go from lacing up my skates and slamming other people into the boards to considering my father's demise. And my possible ascension to the throne.

Just then, the front door of the apartment burst open, and my brother stepped in, every bit as tall, tan, and hand-some as I had always thought of him.

"Deckkie," Lambert called, striding confidently toward me and opening his arms. I stepped into them and hugged my brother tightly. He didn't smell of alcohol, and he didn't seem like he was on anything. Both good signs.

He sat next to me on the couch and shook his head lightly as he said, "So, you're getting the full rundown?"

"Yeah, I think so. It's a lot to take in."

"Did they get to the part yet where I'm not fit to rule?" I looked between him and my parents, waiting for more. Lambert had had his problems, that was true. But I wasn't sure what exactly made him unfit to rule. He looked more fit, healthy, and happy than I'd ever seen him. Plus, he was the one who had been groomed for this his entire life.

I was the one who had left. If anyone was unfit, it had to be me.

"Lamb, we just think it might be best," my mother said.

"For the kingdom?" Lambert asked. I got the sense they'd had this talk many times already.

"For you," my mother said. "For everyone."

Dad sighed heavily and sank back into the cushions of the couch.

"Maybe we can talk about this later?" Mom suggested, rising and taking my father's hand. "Erik, honey, you need to rest."

She turned to us. "You boys catch up. This has been a lot of excitement for your father. We'll see you at dinner."

Lambert stood and gestured toward the hallway. "Wanna see what they've done with your rooms since you moved out? I made your bed chambers into a naked room."

"No, you didn't. That's from a movie."

We walked down the hall, and Lambert grinned. "Doesn't make it less funny." He pushed open the door to my old rooms and ushered me inside like I was a guest. And the second I stepped through, it was like stepping back in time. As we stepped into the bedroom, the only room I'd been allowed to decorate myself, the first thing I saw was the giant poster of Stephano Mizzoni, geared up in his goalie pads, hovering in front of the net at the Wombat Arena—like a demon and a hero all in one.

There were other posters too, all of them hockey play-ers. My childhood idols. But there were also the things I had not chosen—the ceremonial garments hanging on the wall, the typical young royal kit I'd been made to don whenever we were out on official business. I'd hated it then, and even now, something inside me revolted at the sight of those medals gleaming under the soft bedroom light.

I sank onto the small bed in the corner, running my fingers over the unfamiliar duvet. They had changed a few things, but mostly, it was the same room I'd lived in until I was ten.

"Lambert, you've got to explain everything to me," I said finally. "I really don't know why I'm here. I just know that Dad's sick, the kingdom is in trouble, and someone blew up my truck—which, by the way, I really liked."

"Yeah, there's a lot more to the story," Lambert said. "But I don't think this is where we should talk about it."

"My childhood bedroom isn't the right setting for this information?" I felt my face tug up into a half-smile.

"Not by a long shot." Lambert looked around once more, like he was giving me a moment to absorb it all, then nodded toward the door. I followed him as he led me out of the royal residence and into another wing—one I had explored as a child but barely remembered.

He pushed open yet another door, revealing a well-appointed apartment, which I assumed belonged to him. Lambert gestured to a low, comfortable-looking couch against one wall, facing a very large television mounted above a sleek console.

"It wasn't easy, but I get all the Wombats games on that thing," he said, already digging through the fridge. He came up with two beers and walked back across the room, handing one to me.

I raised it toward him hesitantly. "I thought you were in recovery?"

Lambert grinned. "I'm good with alcohol. Just nothing stronger."

"So, you're probably wondering why you've been summoned here."

"Yeah." I cracked the beer open and took a long sip.

"So, Dad had an incident a couple months ago. And it set off alarms about succession."

"An incident?"

Lambert went on to explain that Dad had collapsed at a palace event, attended by only a few members of the public. They thought they had properly debriefed everyone about the importance of keeping the event secret, but speculation had still begun to spread about the state of succession in Murdan.

Dad's illness had never been acknowledged publicly, and still wasn't, but whispers of instability were starting to make the rounds.

Unfortunately, at that same time, Lambert had been on vacation on the other side of the island—where he had supposedly been using "extracurricular medical supplies" in less-than-prescribed ways, according to Murdan's premiere salacious gossip rag. Lambert had long ago been dubbed the "Playboy Prince." That was his official nickname in the media. When he was in his early teens, there had been real problems. He had been put in a recovery program and deemed an addict. And since then, he had been in and out of the rehab center.

Just after my father's "incident," he'd been put back into rehab. And that had brought unwanted public attention to the state of the succession. It was widely believed Lambert was unfit to rule—something that had suddenly taken on far more importance, now that our father's health was in question.

And that was when the quest to locate me had ramped up.

There had always been speculation about the other Murdan prince. But my parents had done a good job hiding my whereabouts, allowing me to live an unfettered, unwatched life. Changing my last name had been a big part of that, and allowing my uncle Jericho to raise me had been equally important.

But clearly, I had been identified, since my truck had recently exploded.

"Your secret life can't be secret anymore," Lambert said.

"Yeah. I got that."

"The question is—do you want to be king?" Lambert stared at me, the question hanging between us.

If he was unfit to be king, I was the definition of the word. At least he had been in royal life for the last decade. I had been in another world. I wasn't up on current affairs, I didn't know who our allies were or who our enemies might be. I hadn't been paying attention at all. And I liked it that way. "No," I said simply. "I don't want to be king. I don't want any of this."

"I figured." Lambert gave me a grim smile.

"So, what do we do?"

"Honestly? I have no idea. Mom and Dad have made up their minds, and most would say there is no challenging the will of a king. Maybe we can figure something out."

Lambert and I figured absolutely nothing out that night. Mom called his apartment and canceled dinner—Dad wasn't feeling up to it. So we ate in his rooms, drank more and talked. And it was so good to be with my big brother again, even if he did insist on calling me Deckkie.

I told him about Lizzy, and he seemed to understand how confusing the whole thing had been. Maybe he understood more than that.

"So where is she now?" he asked as darkness gleamed outside the windows of his apartment.

"I don't know. Wherever all the spies live around here, I guess," I laughed, though I didn't find myself amused at all. Instead, I felt sort of sick. And tired. And just... really, really sad.

"So you really like her?"

"I mean... like is kind of an inadequate word, I think. We were best friends growing up, only I didn't realize it was her until we were practically back here again."

"You were in love with her when you were little?" Lambert asked.

"It was nothing as mature as that," I said, thinking. "She just... She was my reality. She was my childhood. She was my friend." It hurt to think about Eliza, the little girl I had loved as a boy. And it hurt to think of her as Lizzy, the friend I had now lost.

"Well, it isn't like she's gone anywhere," Lambert said. "What's stopping you from pursuing something now?"

"Oh, I don't know. Maybe the fact that I'm supposed to become king?"

"Have you learned nothing from Mom and Dad?"

"What do you mean?"

"Haven't you seen the way they look at each other? They're completely in love. That's why Dad is such an amazing ruler. Because he's not doing it alone. He has a trusted partner."

I thought about that. When I had trusted Lizzy, it had felt good. Like I had a partner. But maybe she was too close to all of this to be a partner now.

Lambert suddenly pulled out his phone, scrolling through photos. He turned the screen to face me, and I saw a picture of a woman, smiling serenely—a very pretty woman, with dark hair and dark eyes.

"This is Celeste," Lambert said in a voice I had never heard him use before. "We're going to get married."

CHAPTER 30
LIZZY

NEEL AND THE CLOSET.

I WATCHED DECLAN WALK AWAY, understanding that this was a definitive line between us. He was returning to his position as prince, and I was a royal guard. Nothing more.

Whatever we had shared in the time that we had both worked for the Wombats in Wilcox, Virginia was over. I needed to remind myself of that. I needed to remember it.

I left the palace proper and walked down the narrow streets inside the palace complex to the long, low building I called home. Because my mother and I both worked for the monarchy, we had always lived here, on the palace grounds. Our home was a small, two-bedroom villa inside the palace gates. And as I unlocked the front door and stepped inside, the familiar scent of Mom's traditional island cooking lofted toward me, embracing me like an old friend.

"You're back." Mom stepped from the kitchen, where

she spent most of her time when she wasn't at Her Majesty's side.

"I'm back. What are you making? That smells amazing," I said.

"I knew you'd be back today. The queen told me so. And I figured I should make your favorite dish."

She stepped close, pulling me into a hug, and the familiarity and comfort there nearly made me cry.

Mom held me at arm's length, her sharp eyes scanning my face, missing nothing. "And what has happened? Something is wrong."

So many things were wrong. But I couldn't tell my mother, could I?

"Come sit and have some coffee, and you can tell me."

It seemed so simple. A cup of coffee. Tell my mom. Maybe it was that simple.

I sank into the familiar armchair that faced the kitchen, but was really part of the tiny family room nestled at its side. Mom brewed coffee on the stovetop using the pour-over method she had always used, then set a mug in front of me, wiping her hands on the apron around her waist before sitting and looking at me expectantly.

"So. You have spent some time with the prince. Your old playmate. And I expect that has brought up some feelings, no?"

I narrowed my eyes. "What do you mean?"

"Eliza, it has never been a secret that you and the prince were close as children. And it was never a secret to me that you might have been closer than you shared with anyone. I know how a young girl's heart can yearn, and I also know that yearning for a prince is a pointless endeavor."

I didn't like these words. But that didn't make them untrue.

"I am not yearning for a prince," I told her. Maybe I was. But I didn't think of him as a prince. I thought of him as Declan, a hockey player. A very complicated hockey player.

"I can see it in your eyes," my mother said, leaning back and crossing her hands over her stomach as she lounged in the chair. She had always been like this—seeing more than I wanted her to and passing judgment. That was the part I hated. Maybe she knew me better than I knew myself, but I didn't like to think she arrived at every conclusion before I'd had a chance to get there.

"Well, all of that is over now," I told her. "I'm back, so I assume I'll be getting another mission shortly."

My mother's eyebrows rose, then lowered as she considered me. She was privy to the deepest inner workings of the royal family and often knew things before anyone else.

"You know, I think romantic relationships are rather pointless," she mused. "But that's just because they've never worked out for me."

She tilted her head, studying me. "I fear I've doomed you."

"Just because you've never been successful at love doesn't mean I won't be," I told her, more to assuage any guilt she might feel than because I thought I had any real chance at finding true love.

"It's not that. It's your place." Her voice softened, but

the weight of her words didn't. "You were born a servant, and loving a prince is pointless."

There it was. The real truth of my relationship with Declan.

He would always be above me, and there was nothing I could do to change my place in the world. No matter how many commendations I received, I would still be part of the serving class.

I moped the rest of the evening, eventually going to bed in my childhood bedroom and dreaming of a prince who would never be mine.

At breakfast the next morning, my mother asked if I had enjoyed myself in the United States.

"I was just happy I could be there to protect him," I told her.

Mom leaned forward. "Protect him? Were there dangers to the prince? In the US?"

"Yes. There were men after him, and his truck blew up." I thought everyone here must have known that by now.

My mother shook her head. "How did these people even find the prince?"

"I have no idea. I thought you might know."

"Nothing has changed. The prince's identity was secret. No one spoke of him. It was as if he never existed. And no one knew the king was ill. That was a very tightly kept secret. It still is."

I doubted very much that a tiny island country would completely forget that a second prince had been born to their rulers. Especially since Declan had been home to visit since moving to the US, his identity was closely guarded and protected. And only someone very close to the palace would have been able to find him. But it certainly wouldn't be impossible.

"There were definitely attempts on the prince's life when I was in Virginia," I told my mother.

"If that is true, then there is a leak somewhere in the palace." She said it serenely, but my feelings at learning this were far from serene.

"You think there's an informant inside the palace? Someone with antimonarchist loyalties?" I stood.

"I didn't say that, Eliza. But it's possible. We should take this to your supervisor and to the king."

She was right. I needed to figure out who Declan and his family could trust—and who they could not. Just because Declan and I did not have a future together did not mean I didn't care for him, for his safety. "Mom, I have to go. I'll see you later."

I headed for the office of the King's Guard, which was situated at the back of the palace. I badged myself in, wearing my standard uniform—black pants, a button-down shirt, and low, functional heels. It was the outfit I had worn every day since being indoctrinated into the King's Guard. Except, of course, when I was on a mission.

I got nods and handshakes welcoming me home. By now, everyone inside the palace compound knew that the prince was back and that I had accomplished my mission.

"I think Neel wants to see you," said Abby Dooley, one of the other female guards.

"I was just heading in that direction," I told her. I straightened my ponytail and knocked on Neel's door.

"Come in," he called. I stepped inside.

"Lizzy, it's so good to see you. Well done," he said, waving me to a chair across from his desk.

I sat. "Thank you, sir. I did want to ask you, though—"

"It can wait." He interrupted me, shuffling papers on his desk and immediately moving on. "I have a new mission for you. You can take a couple of days to settle in and get your bearings, but I need you as soon as you're ready for another undercover mission. In Luxembourg."

"So soon?" My stomach twisted at the thought of leaving again. My appetite for undercover missions had soured. I wanted time at home, to be with my mother. To be with Declan, even if only because I couldn't imagine being far away from him yet.

"You're the best. As soon as you're ready."

"I had a couple of questions about this last mission first." I said.

"Yes, your debrief is scheduled for later this morning. We can talk then."

"But, sir—as you know, there were several attempts on the prince's life and I'm concerned that there might be some kind of leak."

Neel's eyes widened and he dropped the papers he was shuffling. "If there were attempts on the prince's life, why wasn't that information shared with us?" He frowned at me. I felt as if an enormous spotlight had been pointed directly at me. Was I in some kind of trouble? It had been shared.

"I filed my reports each night," I said. "Using the secure protocols you sent me with." I had been up late every night, accessing the portal through which I could make my daily reports. I knew I had done my job exactly as specified. The reports went directly to Neel.

Neel typed into his desktop computer, frowning. "Lizzy, there's nothing here. These are the reports you sent me—nothing about attempts on the prince's life."

"That doesn't make sense. I filed at least three reports a day. We were assaulted in a parking lot... his truck blew up!"

"I see all of your reports, but nothing marked priority." He looked at me grimly. "If any of them had mentioned what you just told me, they would have been marked. And action would have been taken. These reports came directly to me, didn't they?"

"Yes, sir. That's what we arranged before I left."

"Then there is something amiss. This is very odd." He raised an eyebrow, typed something into his computer and stood. It did seem odd. It had seemed odd at the time, back in Virginia. I'd followed protocol and the office hadn't ever followed up.

Neel marched around his desk. "This is very concerning, Lizzy," he said. "Come with me." I barely kept up as he stormed down the hallway. But then—he stopped. Turned. Backtracked. Finally, he yanked open a door and shoved me inside.

Before I could ask what was happening, the door was

shut and bolted.

"Sir?!" No answer. I turned, staring at the small space I had just been thrown into. Brooms, cleaning supplies, a few stacks of crackers and a utility sink.

I was locked in a closet.

At first, I worked on opening the lock, but with the bolt thrown from the outside, I knew there was little chance of getting that to work. I was trying to maintain a professional demeanor. I was at work, after all. Though this situation was slightly…unusual.

I reached for my phone, remembering only as I came up empty that I'd turned it in at security when I'd accessed the palace this morning. Following protocols. No one kept their devices inside the palace complex except the royal family.

"There has to be something in here I can use," I assured myself, wandering the perimeter of the small closet, searching for…what? A magical key? After an hour of doing my best to stay calm and channel action heroes I'd seen in movies, I resorted to panic.

"Help!" I screamed it, hoping someone would be walking by, investigate.

The thing was, I'd never been down this hallway before. I wasn't sure quite where I was, or how many people traversed this route daily. The reason Declan and I had held such incredible games of hide and seek was because the palace was practically a labyrinth. It was such a twisted warren of hallways and corridors I sometimes wondered if a madman had designed the place.

"Help me!" I screamed until my voice was hoarse, but no one came. At least I had light in there. If I was locked in a tiny dark closet, it would be so much worse. Finally, I sank to the floor, my back against the wall. Someone would find me, I was sure. I tried to calm myself and let my mind work on this new problem.

Was Neel the leak? Had he put me here to prevent me telling anyone else of his betrayal? That had to be it. He was the one who'd received those reports.

I had to get out of here. I had to. The royal family might be in danger. Would Neel really do anything to hurt them? To hurt Declan?

I had to escape. "Help!!" I screamed, banging my heels on the door that simply would not budge.

CHAPTER 31

DECK

IF PAPER TOWELS COULD TALK.

WAKING up in my old bedroom was confusing at first. The last time I'd visited, they'd treated me as a proper guest, putting me up in the guest quarters in a different wing of the palace. But that was when they were maintaining my disguise—I was not the prince, just a visitor of some import.

Now, there was no reason to hide me. I was to be the king, after all. (So they shoved me back into my old twin-sized bed, where my feet now hung off the end. Of course.)

"A formal announcement will be made in the next week," Dad was saying at breakfast. "And we will hold the coronation ceremony shortly after." He nodded at both Lambert and me, and I did my best to keep the horror I felt at his statement from my expression.

"So soon?" Lambert asked.

"I see no need to delay," Dad said. "Deckkie is home, and he should assume responsibility as soon as possible to ensure a peaceful transition." I focused on my scones, not wanting to see how this statement might hurt my brother's feelings. There was no talk of the potential for him to ascend, and I gathered those discussions were long past. Everyone in the family had accepted this plan. My coming home had cemented it.

But no one—other than my brother—had asked what I wanted.

I'd had dreams of hockey the night before. That cold ammonia scent of the ice rink that had come to mean home to me, the rush of taking the ice when a crowd waited all around to watch the fight, the feeling of flying that I could never replicate any other way. And Lizzy. Lizzy had been there. And in my dream? She was wearing my jersey.

That's how I knew it was a dream. Lizzy was a professional. She'd never wear a jersey. It would be far too casual. But when I'd first woken up, I felt like I might give just about anything to see her in mine.

That was past though. I needed to look forward. She'd lied to me, she'd betrayed me. She could have just told me what was going on, who she was. Now there was no chance of anything real between us. You didn't build a relationship based on lies.

None of that stopped me from wondering where she was, though, what she was doing. Was she happy? Did her mother still make those delicious fry bakes she used to give us when we were small? If I closed my eyes, I could still taste the brown sugar and the crispy edges... perfection. It all reminded me of Eliza. And something inside me twisted into a tangled mess when I thought of her.

"Did you hear me, Deckkie?" My mother asked, looking at me meaningfully.

I shook my head, sending thoughts of Lizzy scattering. "Sorry, what?"

"I said you'll have fittings this afternoon and all day tomorrow."

"Fittings?" I didn't do a good job hiding the horror in my voice. Nothing sounded worse than getting stuck with needles for two days in a row while standing around trying on clothes. "For what?"

"For your new wardrobe. Kings certainly cannot be seen wearing pink board shorts and T-shirts that say 'pew pew,'" Mom said, wrinkling her nose at me.

Lambert was grinning across the table. "I like your shirt," he whispered loudly enough for them to hear.

"Of course you do." Dad rolled his eyes.

"I guess you can have it when they make me wear… What will I have to wear every day, then?" I tried to imagine Dad's normal wardrobe. This morning he was wearing a robe and looking only slightly less tired than yesterday.

"Proper slacks and tailored shirts. Ties," Mom said. "Cufflinks."

"Ties?" I moaned. I hated ties. There was no worse invention. "Can I pass some kind of royal edict that no one ever has to wear ties again?"

"I think you'll find, son, that there are far more impor-tant issues demanding your attention once you're the sovereign head of our nation." Dad did not seem amused.

"Of course, sir." I struggled to sit up taller, feeling like every word from my family was another weight piled onto my shoulders, pressing me down. I hadn't realized how good I had it. All I wanted was to be back in Wilcox, preparing for a game. Or even dropping trou for Lizzy's calendar. It was all so much better than this.

We finished breakfast, and Lambert and I headed out for a walk on the beach. Naturally, we were closely tailed by five security guys in tailored short-sleeved shirts, an annoyance I supposed I'd need to get used to.

"So," he said. "Settling in?"

"No." I practically spat the word. "I don't want any of this."

He nodded. "It's a lot."

I stopped walking when my feet hit the water, and for a moment I let the cool, clear water pool around my ankles as the sea filled my vision from horizon to horizon on either side. "God, it's gorgeous. You forget."

"Do you?" Lambert asked wistfully.

"That was insensitive. I'm sorry." He'd never been away from Murdan. He wouldn't know if one forgot its beauty.

"A few years ago, I might have been jealous," he said softly. "But now?" He shook his head.

"What do you mean?"

"I love it here, Deck. It took me years of fighting to realize that this is where I'm meant to be. This is what I'm meant to do."

"Stand on the beach with your miserable little brother?"

He smiled at me, a calm benevolence I'd never seen from him emanating. He looked...regal. "Something like that."

A thought occurred to me. "Lambert… do you want to be king?"

He hesitated, keeping his gaze trained on the horizon, the bright blue of the Caribbean Sea making every second feel like an eternity. "I do," he said softly. "But I've accepted Dad's decision. I've made a name for myself for all the wrong things. It's too late now."

I stared at him. This was the answer. Lambert wasn't the same out of control kid he'd been. This version of Lambert, the one that was in love with a beautiful woman? The one who stood here telling me he had no ambitions to leave our tiny country? He should be king.

"What about Celeste?" I asked.

A smile pulled his tanned cheeks wide. "She'll marry me whether I'm a king or a pauper. That's the kind of love I was lucky enough to find." My heart flipped at his words. Luck was right. I envied him.

"Lamb. You should be king."

He shrugged and smiled, so calm I wished I could channel some of whatever newfound Zen he'd found when I was on the ice. "It's too late, Deckkie. I've come to terms with it."

I shook my head and grabbed his shoulder. "It's not too late. I'm not king yet!"

"The kingdom has deemed me unfit."

I frowned at him. Before me stood a man who seemed as fit as any. "Tell me the truth. All those years of rehab… did it work?"

Lambert held my gaze for a second and then dropped it, a secret smile playing on his lips. "Truth?" He asked looking up and scrubbing the back of his neck with a hand.

"Yeah."

"The first time was enough. Scared me straight."

That didn't make any sense, and I told him so. He'd been to rehab at least three times since then.

"Celeste was a counselor there," he said, catching my eyes and then turning his gaze out to sea. "I've known her since I was eighteen. First, she was just helping me, but then… things shifted. Going back was a way to get a week to spend with her, out of the media's eye line. A way to get to know each other without all the pressure."

"And a few months ago? Dad's incident?"

"That was awful timing. I was vacationing on the other side of the island with Celeste—it was when I proposed. But as soon as Dad collapsed, the media swarmed in, and I had to play the part to protect her."

"I don't get it," I admitted.

"This life," Lambert gestured toward the security behind us. "It's not for everyone. I didn't want to force it on her. So I kept her as far from it as I could. Whether that was pretending to need to go back to rehab or renting a villa under an alias and ditching security for a week."

I shook my head. "You dirty dog."

He smiled. "I was just trying to protect her."

"And destroying your own reputation in the process."

His smile grew dimmer. "I succeeded there, that's for sure. And now that it matters, it's too late to fix."

"I'm not king yet," I reminded him.

"But you will be. That's what the people want, what

Dad wants. I ruined my image long ago, and our people have a long memory."

No. I couldn't accept that. He would make a good king, much better than I would. I didn't want it, didn't want to be here at all. Then a thought occurred to me. "It's just PR, Lamb. We just need to rehab your image a little bit."

He raised an eyebrow. "PR, huh? That something you learned in the league?"

"A little bit, yeah. But I know someone else who's great at it." We needed to find Lizzy.

Finding Eliza Canfield was easier said than done.

Together, Lambert and I located her residence—the same place she'd lived with her mother growing up. But neither her mother or Lizzy seemed to be home. Or at least no one answered the door.

"Want me to open it for you, sir?" the closest security guard asked me.

I stared at him. "I can't just go walking into people's houses."

"You can, actually. You're the prince."

I gave him a stern look. "That does not make it right."

"Maybe not, sir. Apologies."

I sighed and turned to Lambert. "She's probably at work anyway. Where do all the King's guards work?"

Lambert shrugged and we both turned back to the security guy who now seemed to be pretending he hadn't heard every word we'd just said.

"What's your name?" I asked him.

"Stuart," he said.

"Where do the King's guards work, Stuart?" I asked.

"This way, sirs." He led us back into the palace building, and down a twisting maze of corridors lined with closed doors. Lambert and I followed him, the other security guards trailing behind us, until we came to a stop at a door marked "Neel Wiley. Director of the Kings Guard."

"Neel's in charge, sir," the man said, knocking on the door.

We waited, but no one answered. Finally, Lambert opened the door and we leaned in, but the office was empty. In fact, the desk appeared to have been ravaged by hurried rodents or a man in a rush to get gone. The computer had been taken, the monitor standing askew on the desktop. Papers had sifted to the floor, and the chair was pushed back and stood at a haphazard angle. There were no personal items at all around the office.

"Other ideas?" I asked the guard.

He shook his head. "Sorry, no. I don't report to Neel."

Lambert and I gazed around the office again and then at one another. Footsteps echoed out in the hall and another guard hurried by in dark slacks and a button-down shirt.

"Excuse me," I called, drawing the man's attention.

His eyes took in my pink shorts and casual T-shirt, and a look of derision crossed his face. But then he lifted his gaze to mine and recognition seemed to dawn.

"Your highness," he said, nodding to me and then to Lambert.

"Yeah, hi. Thanks. Um, do you know this Neel guy?"

"Yes sir. He's my boss."

"Any idea where he might've gone?" I looked up and down the long empty hallway.

"I saw him earlier, sir. He had his computer and said he had a very important mission. He was heading for the helipad."

"Huh," Lambert said. "I guess he won't be much help then."

I shrugged. "Do you know Lizz—er, Eliza Canfield?"

"Yes sir."

"Seen her today?"

"No sir." The guy looked half terrified and didn't seem like he was going to be any use at all.

"Okay, thanks."

He nodded and bowed, and then began backing down the hallway away from us.

"You're going to run into something," I called. "Just walk normally." He didn't listen, instead, continued heading backward, bumping into the wall and then redirecting himself like a pinball.

People were crazy.

"Okay, so if you were Lizzy, where would you be?" Lambert asked me.

"Probably organizing something, kicking someone's ass, or lifting weights." Thinking of Lizzy gave me a warm little buzz I didn't want to examine too closely.

"Okay, Stuart, where's the gym the guards use?" Lambert asked our guide.

"This way." He led us down yet another long winding massive corridor.

"This place is enormous," Lambert said looking surprised.

"Haven't you explored it all by now?" I asked him. "You've been here your entire life."

"I have better things to do than wander hallways," Lambert said. "It occurs to me that maybe we need better custodial services though." He pointed in front of us where a massive pile of paper towels spewed from beneath one door. It looked as if each towel have been shoved out underneath the door and they were accumulating into an enormous pile.

"That's weird," I said. "Maybe it's a mouse?"

"That should not be there. Sorry, sirs." Stuart pulled his walkie talkie from his belt. "Custodial services to corridor ten," he barked.

We had just passed the door when I thought I heard a muffled sound. I turned back and listened, certain I heard a voice.

"Do you hear that?" I asked Lambert, who stopped and turned back toward the door.

"Hear what?" Lambert said.

"I swear I heard a muffled voice calling for help."

"Do you think all those paper towels might be calling for help?" Lambert asked me. I was about to hit him when the sound came again, and it was definitely the word 'help.' It was definitely a woman's voice. In fact, it was a voice that had become so familiar to me that I heard in my dreams.

"Lizzie?" I called back.

The door responded by banging loudly.

I turned to Stuart. "Someone's in there." I tried the handle, but the door didn't budge.

"Help!" Lizzy's voice came again. "Help, I'm locked in!"

"Lizzy, hang on," I called back, my heart trying to beat out of my chest to get to her. Why was Lizzy locked in a closet?

Stuart pulled a ring of keys from his belt and began shuffling through them, finally inserting one and opening the bolt on the door. He wrenched the handle and pulled the door open. On the other side stood Lizzy, eyes wide and chest heaving, and more beautiful than I'd ever seen her.

"You're safe!" she said, and then she hurtled herself into my arms.

I caught her, everything in the universe aligning as I held her close to me, our hearts pressed together. "Yeah," I said. "Why were you in the closet?"

Lizzy stiffened in my grip, probably realizing we had company. She stepped back, straightening her ponytail. "Uh, hello. Hi. Sorry. Oh, Your Majesty," she inclined her head to my brother.

"Stop that," I told her, exasperated with all the royalty bullshit. "Why were you in that closet?"

She looked up and down the corridor. "We have to find Neel! We have to hurry!"

CHAPTER 32

LIZZY

KINGLY CONCERNS.

I WAS VERY relieved to be out of the closet. And I don't mean that metaphorically.

It occurred to me that all of the hallways and corridors in the palace—especially in the guard quarters where the offices were—looked the same. If I wanted to call attention to the door hiding my prison, I needed to make it different.

I had very few tools at my disposal. But I did have a lot of paper towels. So, I began shoving them under the door one by one.

It seemed my plan had worked. What I hadn't planned for was the fact that the person who would discover me would be the one person I was trying to avoid.

Still, when I saw Declan's face—when I saw the concern he clearly felt for me—it tugged at my heart. And before I thought better of it, I threw myself at him. I didn't even realize we had an audience until it was too late. I stepped away from him, trying to suppress the rush of blood to my face and the rapid beating of my heart.

"I'm so glad to see you," Declan said softly.

I stepped out of his arms. "Me too," I said. But now, there were more pressing matters at hand. "We have to find Neel," I said, dashing down the corridor ahead of them.

Declan, Lambert, and Stuart followed, trailing me turn by turn through the hallway. Finally, Declan called out, "Lizzy, do you even know where you're going?"

I stopped. Where was I going?

"We have to find Neel," I repeated, more for my own benefit than anyone else's. Maybe there had been some cleaning products in that closet that had messed with my thinking.

Stuart spoke up. "One of the guards told us he saw Neel rushing to the helipad."

The helipad. That wasn't good.

I spun and took off again, angling toward the nearest exterior door that would take us outside. I slammed through it, Declan, Lambert, and Stuart hot on my heels, and together we raced across the lush green lawns of the palace gardens toward the helipad.

I could hear the chopper blades whirring. Which meant Neel hadn't gotten away yet.

Declan and Lambert overtook me—because of course they did. I realized, fleetingly, that all that hockey conditioning probably made Declan really good in a chase. My competitive nature wouldn't let him win, though. I kicked my legs into high gear.

We all arrived at the helipad together, ducking against the downward force of the chopper blades.

Neel was already strapped into the backseat, clearly

waiting for his pilot. Declan ran around to the other side of the helicopter while Lambert stepped up into the passenger compartment.

"Going somewhere?" Lambert asked.

Neel didn't say anything, just looked back and forth between the two princes. Finally, his gaze dropped to me—then past me, to the pilot approaching from the far side of the helipad. It was clear to Neel that he was not going anywhere.

When the helicopter was shut down and we'd explained everything to the pilot, Stuart took Neel into custody, and we marched him toward the royal quarters.

"I think my father might have some questions for you," Lambert told Neel.

Neel alternated between shooting me hard looks and grumbling about monarchies in general.

"Why would you do this, Neel?" I asked him. Neel had been a mentor, a friend. A liar, I realized.

He frowned at Declan and Lambert. "The monarchy has been in place for too long, keeping our nation mired in antiquity. When it looked like King Erik would die and Lambert was in no shape to ascend, it was a perfect opportunity to modernize. We didn't expect you to make it back," he told Declan.

That was offending on so many levels. Neel hadn't believed I could protect the prince? "Why did you send me if you wanted to kill Declan? You knew I'd defend him with my life."

"I honestly didn't think that would be enough," Neel admitted. "Figured you'd be too busy pretending to be a PR consultant to actually keep an eye out for threats."

"So rude," I said under my breath.

"Who would be in charge?" Lambert asked. "Just out of curiosity." I knew he was asking in case there were other members of the current security force or palace staff that had been working with Neel.

My former boss chose that moment to seal his lips, narrowing his eyes at Lambert. I knew he wouldn't be able to stay silent forever. I was just glad we'd caught him before the group he was working with could attempt to mount an even more dangerous offensive against the crown.

But when we entered the palace again, he quieted completely. Perhaps he realized that his fate was sealed, no matter how he felt about the monarchy.

"I've got this," Lambert said, stopping Declan and me in the hallway just ahead of the doors to the royal apartments. "Stuart and I can handle it."

"You sure?" Declan asked.

"Yeah, I'm sure. You have some things to discuss with Lizzy."

Lambert's eyebrows moved up and down in a very suggestive way, and I really wanted to know what he and Declan had been talking about.

"That's true," Declan said. He turned to me. "Lizzy, do you have a few minutes?"

My heart jumped. I told myself that this would surely be about the crown, the treason we had just uncovered, or his potential ascension to the throne. It wouldn't have anything to do with us.

Don't hope for anything else, I warned myself. I took a deep breath and faced Declan as we sat on a bench just outside the entrance we'd come through.

"Lizzy, I wondered if you might be willing to put on your PR hat a little bit longer." That was definitely not what I had been expecting him to say.

"I don't really have a PR hat. You know that."

"I think we both know more about PR than we used to," Declan said.

"Doesn't make either of us qualified for anything," I told him.

He laughed. "That's true. I am only qualified to play hockey." He smiled and rubbed a hand across one side of his beard. My eyes followed the movement, and I hated myself for wishing I could feel that softness again.

But there was a separation between us now. A distance that needed to stay in place.

He was royalty.

I... was not.

"What do you need PR for?" I asked.

"It's not for me. It's for my brother. I need to show the people that he's fit to rule. He's had some... PR crises in the past."

"No shit."

"Yeah. But the thing is—that was all spin, too."

"What do you mean?" I asked.

It was common knowledge that the older prince had been in and out of rehab most of his adult life.

"What if everything you think you know about Lambert is wrong?" Declan asked.

I stared at him. "That would be a pretty fantastic story."

"Well, then you're gonna love this," Declan said.

And then he told me a story. A fantastic one.

When he was done, my mind was spinning.

Everything the people of Murdan believed about their prince was a lie. And it was a lie all in the name of love.

What better story was there than that?

Sure, the prince had allowed himself to take on an image that was somewhat scandalous. But the reality was that he had successfully protected someone he loved.

And done no real harm.

The true heir was fit to rule, after all.

That was a happy ending.

And the people of Murdan would certainly embrace it—if it was put to them the right way.

"I think we need to change Lambert's image gradually," I told Declan.

"We don't have much time, Lizzy," he said. "They've got me in fittings this afternoon. And tomorrow."

"What does that have to do with anything?" I asked.

Declan gave me a look. "Only that they're pretty set on me being king."

I exhaled sharply. "All right," I said. "Then we'll have to work fast."

CHAPTER 33

DECK

FINDING THE RIGHT TREE IS IMPORTANT.

FOR A MOMENT, neither of us said anything, and we both sat still, our backs to the palace, the warmth of the Murdan sun beating down on our skin. There were so many things I wanted to say to her, so much I needed to say. But I wasn't sure she'd want to hear any of it. Still, I thought about my brother, about his confidence and security about the woman he loved. I had to try.

"I remember you, Eliza," I began, turning to face the woman I loved. Her hair was pulled back into the tight ponytail she favored when she was working, and her dark expressive eyes caught mine.

She looked confused. "I mean… I would hope so. We came out here together. It's only been a minute or two. Are you feeling okay?" She squinted at me, and I couldn't tell if she was kidding or not.

"I remember you from when we were kids."

"Oh. That."

"Yes, that. I remember all of it. And I remember how I felt about you then," I continued.

"Oh." Lizzy dropped my gaze, her fingernails suddenly catching her attention.

"I remember that with you was the only place I felt like a regular kid, a guy with other things to think about besides all of this." I waved my hand at the extensive grounds and the building behind me. "You were fun and brilliant and sweet," I went on. "Man, I had the biggest crush on you."

Lizzy looked up at me through her lashes. "Yeah?"

"Totally. That's why I kissed you. Do you remember?"

She straightened. "A girl always remembers her first kiss, Declan."

I grinned, I liked believing she'd replayed that moment over the years. It was pretty chaste, just a peck on the mouth really, barely a graze. But it had come from the heart of a nine-year-old kid who had no idea what he was doing. But who really, really liked the girl in front of him.

"It was right around here somewhere, wasn't it?" I asked her, standing and striding toward the tree I thought was the one beneath which I'd given her that kiss.

She shook her head, sending her ponytail flying. "It wasn't that one." She grabbed my hand and tugged me to a different tree a few feet away. "It was here."

Lizzy stopped and looked up at me then. We stood almost chest to chest, and I found that my breathing was coming quicker as my heart rate accelerated at the look in her eyes.

"This tree? You sure?"

"What did I just tell you? Girls don't forget these

things." She stared up at me, a challenge in those dark irises.

I waited a beat, giving her a chance to change her mind, and then I answered the challenge. My lips met hers softly at first, testing, being certain this was what she'd meant. And then I gave her a real kiss, pulling her against me—hard—and tasting her tongue with my own. A soft moan escaped her, and the stiffness in my pants grew harder. I pressed it to her for the tiniest hint of relief, and it elicited another breathy sound.

"Nine-year-old me didn't really know what he was doing," I said, taking a break to regain my self-control.

Lizzy's hands were grasping at the skin beneath my shirt, pulling me closer almost desperately. "I'm glad, or I would've been pregnant by eleven," she breathed, fusing her mouth to mine once again.

Things escalated, and as I cupped her bottom and Lizzy lifted her leg to wrap around my hip, I remembered where we were. Who we were.

"Not here." I pulled away, keeping her hand firmly in my own, as I tugged her toward the palace doors. We went back inside, and I ducked through the first doorway I recognized, into the guest suites I'd occupied last time I'd visited. I locked the door behind us, then spun Lizzy around, pinning her against the door.

"Lizzy, I don't want to lose you."

"This isn't… We're not…You're…" she was gasping these words as I devoured the skin of her throat, my hands working up and down her torso and teasing her nipples. "I can't talk while you do that," she finally managed, pulling away.

"Do you want to talk?" I asked this question of her lips mostly, since I couldn't drag my eyes away—they were so lush, swollen from our kisses.

"Not right now," she said, her words sharp as she tugged me from the door to the long low couch in the center of the room, pulling her shirt off with the other hand. I pulled my own T-shirt over my head, falling to the couch on top of her and resuming my assault on her mouth.

She tasted like mango and salt and so much like home it almost cracked my heart in two.

There were things we needed to say, things that needed to be cleared up immediately. But Lizzy had worked her hand down the waistband of my shorts and was stroking my length with hard, firm pulls, and my mind was shorting out.

I gave up, or gave in, letting my body take over as my mind went on hiatus. Lizzy's pants were off a moment later, and her panties followed shortly after. She'd already told me she was on the pill, and neither of us had found time for anyone else, I didn't think. I pulled her onto my lap, my cock an eager third party jutting up between us.

The position put her breasts at eye-level, which was fucking perfect. I leaned in, taking the right nipple in my mouth, sucking hard, then releasing and moving to the other side. Lizzy responded by fisting my cock again. Relentlessly.

Then she raised herself up, positioning her entrance just at the throbbing head of my cock, and lowered herself in the most infuriatingly slow movement I'd ever been tortured with. It was awful. It was amazing. I never wanted it to end.

My hands found her hips and guided her into a rhythm as I leaned back into the cushions of the couch and watched her work above me. Her strong arms were braced on my shoulders, her head thrown back, and her breasts jutted out before her, bouncing with every thrust. I knew I'd be replaying this memory over and over in my more… private moments.

And the feeling… I was on the edge of exploding, but kept pulling myself back. I didn't want it to end. Lizzy was too perfect and I feared maybe this was just some random act of kindness, maybe it would never happen again. Therefore, it needed to last as long as possible.

"Oh God," Lizzy breathed over me, "Declan, I'm gonna…"

"Nope. Stop." I lifted her off me and set her on her feet. Her knees buckled a little, but then she found her footing. And, evidently, her anger.

"What the fuck?"

"Not yet."

"What? Declan, I was like a second away from—"

"I know." I stood and took her hand, pulling her to the bedroom. "I didn't want you to go yet."

"But… Declan," she moaned.

"I'll take care of you," I assured her. "But just in case this never happens again, I want to make it last. It has to be really good."

"It was really good," she cried, flopping backward onto

the bed, every muscle standing in beautiful relief along her toned limbs.

"It'll be better," I promised.

"Don't make me kill you," she whispered as I covered her body with mine, notching myself at her entrance again.

"I'll just tease you the tiniest bit first," I said, sliding in an inch or so and then halting, even though it nearly killed me to stop.

"Come on," she groaned, trying to thrust upward.

"Patience."

"I don't have that," she moaned, writhing beneath me, trying to get friction where she wanted it.

I slid in an inch farther.

"Oh god, you're going to kill me."

I had been thinking the exact same thing, but I didn't accelerate my pace. Instead, I slid in inch by torturous inch, and Lizzy's body clenched and shivered with each little bit I gave her, trying to pull me in, to get closer still.

Finally, I was fully seated, and I swear to god I thought I might actually cry, it felt so fucking good. Instead, I just let myself savor it for a long moment, holding myself still and savoring the way Lizzy's body clutched and pulsed at my cock.

"If you don't start moving, I swear to fucking-"

I covered Lizzy's naughty mouth with my hand and began rocking in a slow, steady rhythm.

"Oh," she said, finally sounding agreeable. I removed my hand, getting better purchase on the bed next to her head. I was at the very end of my control, but there was no way I was going to go first.

"Oh," she agreed again as I rocked. "Oh, god, oh yeah, oh please…" I felt Lizzy's orgasm at the same time her words became utter nonsense and her arms tightened around my shoulders like a set of steel bands. Shit, the woman was strong!

Her channel milked my cock as she came, and that threw me completely over the edge, a tingling starting low in my spine and rushing up my nervous system until stars were blasting behind my eyelids and I might have been speaking—or maybe screaming—in tongues. The sensations went on and on, skittering through my limbs, unfurling deep inside my abdomen, spiraling through my chest until I finally went limp, pushing my weight to one side of Lizzy.

It might have been a second or perhaps several hours later that I opened my eyes to look at her.

"Fuck," she whispered.

"Right?"

"But Your Highness, we really do need to talk."

That line right there unsexified the whole situation for me. "Yep. Okay." I headed for the bathroom, cleaned up and got dressed. After Lizzy had done the same, she met me in the sitting room.

"I hate it when you call me Your Highness," I told her.

She rolled her eyes. "It's appropriate. You're royalty. I'm your servant."

"Ew, no. Not unless we're just playing some kind of fun game." I wiggled my eyebrows at her.

"Declan, what are we doing?" Lizzy looked upset

suddenly, and my heart dropped. No, I didn't want her upset.

"We're… I don't know. We're being together?"

"That's impossible, though," she said. "You're going to be king. You can't be having a fling with a guard." She shook her head, and her hands went to her ponytail, which she smoothed and refastened.

"What if I wasn't king?"

"I'm not sure it matters," she said. "What do you mean, though?"

I reminded her about Lambert, about his image problem, his PR needs.

"And you really think I can help?"

"I think we can do it together."

"I don't think a wombat and a calendar are the answer to this one," she said.

"Wombats help everything," I suggested. "But maybe you're right. Something else then."

In the next couple hours, Lizzy and I got to planning, interrupted once when Dad called to hear Lizzy's input on Neel's betrayal. We ordered dinner into the guest quarters, and spent the night there. Before we finally went to sleep, I texted my brother.

> Declan: Lambie, we've got it all figured out. Operation PR begins tomorrow. Meet us on the front lawn tomorrow at ten. Bring Celeste.

CHAPTER 34
LIZZY

DAY OF PLAY.

THE NIGHT I spent with Declan in the palace felt like a dream.

Not just because it had been amazing, but because it seemed like the only way we could truly be together—if at all—was in my dreams. For now, I was focused once again on helping him. He didn't want to be king, and selfishly, I thought that maybe if he wasn't king, there might be a chance for us.

So, I dedicated myself to Declan's ridiculous PR ideas. And honestly, the plan we'd come up with might just work.

We met Lambert the next morning on the royal lawn, where a small stage had been erected, and we had invited local press. There weren't a lot of major news outlets in Murdan, but there were plenty of influencers who had a surprising amount of reach.

"What's going on?" Lambert asked, looking around at the citizens and reporters milling about.

We might have leaked a little hint about today's festivities on some of the palace's social media channels last night.

"This is step one in your PR rehabilitation campaign," Declan told his brother.

"You ready for your briefing?" I asked.

Lambert looked skeptical, but he nodded. Just then, a woman stepped up beside him—a tall, dark-haired, dark-skinned woman who might have been in her early thirties.

"Deck, Lizzy, this is Celeste."

The way Lambert changed when she was at his side told me everything I needed to know. He loved her completely. And she was gorgeous, polite, and the way she looked at him told me she loved him just as much.

"It's a pleasure to meet you, Celeste," Declan said, smiling at the woman who clearly had his brother's heart. "Has Lambert told you a bit of the plan?"

"I don't know the plan," Lambert said, opening his hands and shaking his head.

"The plan is this," I told him. "In just a few minutes, you're going to step up and announce the first annual Murdan Day of Play."

"Day of Play?" Lambert looked confused.

"Yes," Declan said. "Every employer in the kingdom will give their employees at least two hours off this afternoon to go to a public park—or come here, to the palace lawn—to play. You and I will be out playing with all the kingdom's children, Mom and Dad will be here, and we will build goodwill with our citizens."

"The big PR plan is to play?" Lambert asked, looking between Declan and me.

"It's just the first step, Lambert," I told him.

"It sounds marvelous to me," Celeste said, smiling.

"I guess it's worth a try," Lambert said. He looked at me. "You're the expert, after all."

I didn't want to tell him the truth—just like I hadn't wanted any of the Wombats players to know I had absolutely no idea what I was doing when it came to PR.

So, I just smiled and nodded.

Within the hour, a patio had been set up for the royal family, with shade and refreshments, and the press and many citizens had gathered in front of the stage to one side of the lawn.

Lambert climbed the stairs and took his spot in front of the microphone, tapping it to see if it was on.

"Men and women of Murdan," he called out, quieting the crowd. "I'm Lambert, son of King Erik and Queen Penelope. You all know I enjoy a good romp as much as the next guy, so I thought it would be fitting for me to be the one to announce Murdan's first annual Royal Day of Play."

The gathered crowd roared—clapping and cheering. Many were taking pictures of Lambert, standing with the royal banners waving in the air behind him.

"This afternoon," Lambert continued, "I hope you'll join us here on the royal lawn, or in one of the many public parks throughout the land, to celebrate and play with your family and friends. Though it's often overlooked, play is an important part of being a whole human."

Declan leaned in toward me. "He's going off script."

"I think it's good," I told him.

Lambert continued, "Though there is such a thing as too

much play, I think having some time off—time to bond with those you love—is what makes us well-rounded people. And so, I'd like to introduce you to a new face here at the palace. The woman I love. This is Celeste."

He gestured for Celeste to join him on the stage, and she did so—seemingly reluctantly.

Despite her hesitation, Celeste climbed the stairs gracefully and stood with poise at Lambert's side.

"They're the perfect royal couple," Declan murmured, leaning close to my side.

His breath tickled my ear, sending a shiver down my spine. But I had to agree with him. They did look regal standing there together as the crowd cheered their welcome to Celeste.

The rest of the day went off without a hitch.

With so many people gathered on the royal lawn, I wasn't sure I had ever seen so many Murdan citizens in one place—except maybe in videos of King Erik's coronation.

Families and children romped and played, vendors lined the streets near the palace selling lemonade and ice cream, and it was a lighthearted, glorious afternoon.

I kept a close eye on the palace's social media accounts, which filled with photos and gleeful posts made by participating citizens.

That evening, Declan invited me to join his family for an early supper.

"Of course you'll go," my mother told me when I asked her whether it was appropriate. "You don't refuse an invitation from the royal family."

"It's only... I think Declan might expect something."

"Expect something?" she asked. "Like what?"

"I don't know. I just… I don't know what we are, where we stand. I don't even know if I have a job anymore, now that Neel's gone."

"We have plenty of time to work all these things out," she said. "For now, go enjoy your success from today. And have dinner with the man you love."

"Mom, I never said—"

It felt silly to deny it.

I did love Declan.

I just didn't see how a real future was possible for us.

There was such an immense chasm between our places here in Murdan.

"Well done," said the king, toasting his sons at dinner.

"Well done, indeed," said the queen, smiling at all of us around the table. "What a wonderful day. And who knew that what our citizens really needed was just a day of play?"

"Lambert knew," Declan said, smiling at his older brother.

"Well, Lambert would know about play," the king said, his voice taking on a stern tone.

I knew that meant we still had work to do. But I wasn't worried.

The way the queen and king had embraced Celeste—

who sat quietly at Lambert's side as we ate—suggested they were open to seeing their older son in a new light.

"Son, how did the fittings go?" the queen asked Declan.

Declan hesitated, and I realized—he hadn't gone to his fittings.

"Yes, well, Mom… I thought we might delay those a bit."

"Whatever for?" The queen looked distressed and put her fork down.

"I just don't feel ready," Declan said.

The queen frowned but relented. "I can try to reschedule for next week, I suppose. Will you be ready then?"

"Yes. Next week would be good. Late in the week."

"Fine," the queen said, taking a sip of wine. "I'll try for Thursday."

Lambert exhaled and looked between his parents, his sudden sigh pulling everyone's attention. He blushed a bit and I wondered what had gotten him flustered when no one had spoken a word. After a long moment, he blurted, "The thing is… I'm going to marry Celeste."

Celeste smiled. "And I'm going to marry you," she said softly. And in that moment, everything in the room changed.

The truth—all of it—was about to come out.

The king leaned back in his chair, shaking his head, before breaking into a deep, booming laugh.

Then, looking at his son, he said, "But don't you see? This changes everything."

CHAPTER 35
DECK

WUV AND MER-WUGE.

FOR THE NEXT TWO WEEKS, my brother's image was revamped from the inside out, and the bulk of the effort happened in our private quarters, where my mother and father got a whole different view of their oldest son.

They talked—something maybe they hadn't spent much time doing before I'd come home and pressed the issue—and Lambert revealed the truth about his relationship with Celeste, and why he'd been willing to be seen as the Playboy Prince for so long.

His image began improving rapidly outside the palace as well.

After the Royal Day of Play, we celebrated the first-ever Knight for a Day.

The palace had a bunch of plastic commendation pins lying around, and Lizzy had the idea to knight common citizens for acts of heroism.

"But I don't understand," my mother had said. "There

are so few opportunities to do anything truly heroic. How many people will actually appear for this?"

"Forgive me for disagreeing, Your Highness," Lizzy said to my mom, "but there are so many opportunities to be an everyday hero.

"For example, when we were in Virginia, I was not doing a very good job. I mean, I was doing a good job as a guard, but Declan didn't know that was my job. He thought I was supposed to be a PR consultant—at which I was terrible.

"But he didn't want to see me fail, so he pitched in, came up with ideas for me, and even offered hands-on help so that I wouldn't lose my job."

"I bet he offered hands-on help," Lambert muttered under his breath before I elbowed him hard in the ribs.

"So you're talking about common heroics," my mother said, nodding at Lizzy.

"Not common," Lizzy clarified. "But everyday. I think that for those we love, we go out of our way and do heroic things every single day. This is an opportunity for people in the kingdom to recognize one another—knighting someone for a day as a way to honor their acts of everyday heroism."

"Exactly. That's exactly what I was going to say," Lambert said, nodding.

"It's exactly what you will say in the press release," Lizzy told him, smiling.

"Well, that sounds lovely," my mother agreed. "Plus, we can finally get rid of all those silly plastic pins."

"Yes," I agreed. "We have so little storage space here in the palace."

My mother made a face at me, and I knew better than to push my luck.

Lizzy's royal PR campaign was working.

Each day, more and more Murdan citizens posted about Prince Lambert—how much they admired him, how interested they were in his relationship with Celeste. People were beginning to speculate about how soon they might be announced officially as the new royal couple.

Mentions of my father's illness were few, and we were working inside channels to shut down speculation on that front.

As far as the people of Murdan knew, there was no coronation in the near future, just a new era of royal openness and more royal activity than there had been in the past.

Despite the rosy outlook for Murdan, I was struggling. I wanted to be playing hockey, to be with my teammates. When John Samuels called one morning to check in, I felt a pang of longing I could only think of as homesickness.

"We miss. you, man," he said.

"I miss you all too. Seems like you're playing pretty well without me, though." That was the worst part of it. Did they even need me?

"Hey, family first. You handle what needs handling. We're just getting by until you get back."

"Nice of you to say."

"It's the truth, brother." John's words soothed the ache

inside me a little bit, and I knew he was right. At least about needing to focus on my family for right now.

When Lizzy's campaign culminated in the announcement of the kingdom's first National Date Night, the citizens embraced it wholeheartedly.

Giant movie screens were erected in public venues around the kingdom, and a romantic film was selected to play far and wide.

The palace lawn was covered with blankets and picnic baskets, couples and families lounging happily together. The royal family had our own spot at the front, discreetly surveyed by our guards, but still among our people.

Lizzy sat beside me, something that made me nearly giddy with happiness. We were not official in any way, but I knew that what I felt for her was real. There was a lot for us to figure out, but that hadn't stopped us from settling into the guest quarters as if they had been offered to us. The quiet evenings I spent with her there only cemented my belief that we were meant to be together.

Nothing had changed since we were children.

Well, a lot had changed—but our hearts were the same, and they knew one another.

"This is very exciting," my mother said, looking at all the people gathered around us, smiling and laughing before the movie began. "Lambert, son, are you feeling all right?"

Lambert did look a little sweaty and somewhat uncomfortable. I hoped he wasn't going to barf like he had at his first royal event as a kid. I wasn't sure why watching a movie would have him so green anyway. The lights around the perimeter of the lawn dimmed slightly, and the movie screen ahead of us flickered to life.

Where I had expected to see the opening credits, my brother's face appeared instead. He wore his royal ceremonial uniform and faced the camera, looking serene and regal.

"Citizens of Murdan, I am so glad to see so many of you have joined us for this first annual National Date Night. Celebrating love is one of the best ways we can demonstrate gratitude, and gratitude—for the little things and the big ones—is one of the best ways to celebrate life. There are hardships. There are situations we wish we could change. But when we practice gratitude for the good things in our lives, it can make some of those problems feel less difficult.

"My love for my country cannot be understated, and that is why I wanted to share a very special event with you.

"You have all met Celeste, the woman I love. The woman to whom I have pledged my heart. And I wanted to share with you that she has agreed to become my bride. My wife."

The lawn erupted into a gleeful cacophony of cheering, clapping, and shouting. In a short span, Lambert had won over the hearts of his countrymen, and they were all rooting for him.

Nothing brings people to your side better than a great love story.

"We haven't chosen a wedding date yet," Lambert continued, "but I hope that you will embrace Celeste as you do the rest of my family and make her feel welcome when you see her out and about.

"Thank you for all of your support and enthusiasm. And now, without further delay, let's enjoy one of the most romantic movies of all time—The Princess Bride."

My parents were staring at Lambert, clearly surprised by his little introduction. The citizens closest to us on the lawn were grinning in his direction, smiling at Celeste, nodding their heads, and offering their congratulations.

"I'm proud of you, son," my father said to Lambert. "You have really stepped up these past couple of weeks. You've brought the country together, too."

My mother and father exchanged a look, and I knew there was a chance they were thinking about the succession. Our PR campaign, after all, had been more about changing their minds than about changing the minds of our fellow countrymen.

Lizzy leaned against me as we watched the movie, laughing at the appropriate parts and clapping when the prince got his bride.

I didn't pay much attention to the film, too focused on the woman in my arms.

My happiness was like a living thing inside me, growing constantly the more time I got to spend with Lizzy. There were things I needed to say to her, questions I needed to ask. I just hoped I could be as brave as Lambert had been these last couple of weeks.

First, though, I needed to find out what my future would hold.

If I had my way, Lizzy would be a part of it.

But if I was to be king, I knew there was a chance we'd

have to say goodbye. Lizzy might not want to live the rest of her life in the spotlight, and I was certainly not going to drag her into it. For now, our time together felt precious and perfect.

CHAPTER 36
LIZZY

CORONATION CONUNDRUM.

ONCE LAMBERT'S public persona was fully rehabilitated and he had the hang of managing it himself, there was less for me to do on that front. I returned to the office of the guard, happy to see Stephanie Long taking Neel's place. She was levelheaded, intelligent, and someone I was sure the realm could trust.

Declan and I spent time together, getting to know each other in our home country as the people we were born to be. But there was a layer of uncertainty between us. I would be sent off soon on a new assignment—though Neel's mission to Luxembourg turned out to be only a ploy to keep me out of his way as he continued to foment anti-monarchist sentiment. It didn't matter anyway, since soon, Declan would become king. There had been no indication that the plan had changed despite Lambert's excellent new image.

At the Queen's insistence, Declan went to his royal fittings, taking Lambert for moral support. I supposed that was the kind of thing men needed when they had to try on clothes for hours at a time. More importantly, I took it as confirmation that Declan intended to ascend the throne.

It was the one thing we didn't talk about. That and our true feelings, but those two topics were so interwoven, we couldn't touch on one without the other coming up. I guessed we were both living in denial, delaying the inevitable.

My feelings for him didn't change. They only deepened.

"And until you tell him how you feel, you'll never be able to say that you really tried," my mother told me repeatedly. "You must be brave."

The thing was, I was brave. I was brave in the face of real, actual, physical danger.

So why was I so scared to tell Declan how I felt about him and what I really wanted?

"The calendar looks incredible," Joey told me when we talked later that night. I'd asked Declan for some time, and was lounging on my bed in my old room, my mother in the den watching television.

"I'm so glad," I told her. I really was. Even if my PR assignment had been fake, it mattered to me that the players I'd come to admire got what they were looking for out of the effort.

"Honestly, these photos are so hot," Joey gushed. "I'm emailing you the PDF, okay? You'll die."

"And is it selling?"

"Like hotcakes," she confirmed.

"And how's Wilma?"

Joey chuckled. "Well, it turns out, wombats are quite the handful. Luckily, this one is already pretty domesticated, though John isn't thrilled when he gets into his hockey gear."

"So, are you and Prince Declan spending a lot of time together?" I'd told Joey the whole truth earlier in the conversation when she'd mentioned Declan's absence from the team. It didn't feel right to keep the secret, and there was little chance the rest of the team wouldn't find out soon enough. For now, I had asked her to keep it quiet.

"We are," I admitted. "But I can't pretend I see a future for us."

"What? Why not? I would think discovering you share a homeland and a past crush would have cemented things!"

"There's the little detail of him being royalty. And my being from the serving class," I reminded her.

"It's not the Dark Ages," she laughed. "Does that even matter?"

I didn't know. "It might. To his family. Maybe to him, though he hasn't admitted it."

"Lizzy, that's ridiculous," Joey said, sounding angry on my behalf. "You're an amazing person—what difference does it make if your family is royalty? Or noble or whatever?"

I sighed. "It's just… it's tradition. It's hundreds of years of things being done a certain way," I told her. "For all I know, Declan's parents have someone in mind for him already."

"Well do they?"

"I don't know." Declan had never mentioned it if they did. Maybe he didn't know?

"I think you should go for it. You guys are perfect together, regardless of class or station or whatever. This isn't Downton Abbey, Lizzy."

But it was pretty darned close.

To the great surprise of most of those in the kingdom, a coronation date was announced. As it was only two days away, the kingdom became a ruckus of preparation and speculation.

I'd stayed with Mom, letting Declan spend time with his family in the lead up to taking his position. He would become king, and I thought I would probably ask Stephanie for an assignment as far away from Murdan as I could get. I could think of no better way to forget that I hadn't gotten what I wanted than to escape.

But my mother's words, and Joey's rang in my ears. I needed to at least tell him how I felt. Then I'd know we really didn't have a chance. If I didn't try, I'd always wonder.

When I texted Declan to ask if he could meet me, he agreed, and he was at my door fifteen minutes later.

"Walk a bit?" I suggested, and he smiled, taking my hand in his.

"I've missed you," he said, leaning in and nuzzling my ear, sending a wave of warmth through me.

"I wanted to give you some space. I know there's a lot going on."

He squeezed my hand, and we headed for the beach. Declan and I walked hand in hand along the shore, the waves creating a rolling soundtrack to accompany my racing heart. We talked about everything and nothing, but the one thing I really needed to say remained unsaid.

"Declan," I finally said, mustering the courage to tell him once and for all how I felt. He turned to face me, that wide smile in place—the one I loved so much. Declan had seemed happy here, though I knew he missed playing hockey.

"I was hoping we could talk a little bit," I said, hesitating as I faced him, the ocean painting a brilliant blue backdrop behind us.

Declan squeezed my hand and laughed. "Lizzy, we've been talking since we got here. I think you know everything there is to know about me by now."

"Right," I said. "But I guess I was hoping we could talk about what happens next."

"The coronation, you mean," Declan said, nodding.

"Right. And other things."

I was about to just lay it out there when Lambert trotted up, red-faced and breathing hard, as if he'd sprinted to find us. "Deck, you need to come home. It's about Dad."

Declan looked at me, worry etched in every line of his face.

"This can wait," I told him.

Declan and Lambert dashed off across the sand, leaving me to contemplate the words I had been about to say.

I texted Declan later that night, asking if everything was okay.

He responded with:

> Yes, everything is great. I'll update you as soon as I can — Mom wants to spend some time as a family, but all is well.

It didn't tell me what I wanted to know at all, but it sounded like the king was okay. For the moment, at least.

The day of the coronation arrived.

I found I didn't want to go. But I had to.

I had been appointed to stand with the queen and king, keeping an eye on the crowd. For me, that was a little closer than I wanted to be to watching the man I loved take on a responsibility that would mean we could likely never be what I wanted us to be. I hadn't found a chance to speak to him, and he hadn't sought me out. Preparations for the coronation had been all-consuming, even in the Guards' office.

That morning, I worked with the other agents to double-check the security of the enormous hall where the coronation would be held. Given that it was inside the palace proper, security had been tight to begin with, but it was doubly so for this momentous event.

The people of Murdan had been told little beyond the fact that King Erik planned to abdicate the throne and that one of his sons would be taking his place. In recent years, the assumption had been that Lambert would be crowned, but with Declan's reappearance, there was quite a bit of whispered discussion about who Murdan's next ruler would be.

My heart was heavy as I checked aisles and seats, ensuring that everything was as it should be.

At the appointed hour, the coronation hall was completely full of citizens, with more clustered in the streets outside the palace gates. Murdan guards and soldiers lined the sides of the great hall, standing at attention in their ceremonial uniforms. Their polished swords gleamed under the golden light cast by the immense chandeliers. At the front of the enormous hall stood a raised platform, upon which sat two thrones—rightfully fit for a king and queen.

I met the royals as they entered from a side door into the small chamber at the back of the hall. When the trumpets began to play the Murdan anthem, I walked behind the king and queen, keeping my eyes on the crowd to ensure their safety. Hand in hand, King Erik and Queen Penelope strode confidently—but slowly—toward the front of the hall. The anthem swelled, the banners overhead swaying gently from the high rafters. The rich, deep blue of Murdan's flag, embroidered with gold, filled every corner of my vision.

At the front of the hall, King Erik turned slowly, his queen on his arm, and they took their places on the throne. The crowd quieted in reverence.

Before the king spoke, both of his sons followed their mother and father up the aisle, their own security detail at their sides. Each was dressed in ceremonial garb, flowing robes draped over their shoulders, the weight of tradition resting heavily on them both. Declan looked more handsome than I had ever seen him. And more... kingly. Untouchable.

When Declan and Lambert reached the front, they flanked their parents and turned to face the gathered citizens. King Erik rose from his seat as one of his guards placed a microphone before him.

"Citizens of Murdan," he called out, his voice steady and strong. "It is with great joy that I address you today, on this day of coronation for a new king."

A hush fell over the room.

"It has been my greatest joy to serve as guardian of this country and its people. The people of Murdan are faithful, strong, and loyal, and I could have asked for no better life than the one I have led. That said, I would like the opportunity to enjoy my family. I see no real reason why a monarch must remain so until their demise. Especially when a capable heir stands ready to take on the duty. So today, I am pleased to pass the crown and scepter to my very capable son."

He looked between his sons, smiling. They each smiled back at him, standing tall before their father.

"Declan, your time here in Murdan has not been as long-lived as your brother's, but the years you spent away have given you a broader understanding of the world at large. I am proud of you, as is your mother, as is your country. That is why I ask you today to accept an important responsibility to your kingdom."

Declan stepped forward, meeting his father's gaze before dropping to one knee. The entire hall held its breath and I felt sick as the man I loved prepared to be elevated far above a station where we might be together.

King Erik lifted the royal scepter and touched it gently to Declan's shoulders before bidding him rise.

"Declan Sinclair MacArthur, I declare you…"

The title that followed was one I had not expected.

"…Prince Regent of Murdan."

I let out a slow breath, trying to steady my heart. I did not understand what was happening. Prince Regent? What did that mean? I understood both words, but I'd been expecting to hear king. My body trembled as Declan rose and stepped back to his mother's side.

"Lambert Edward MacArthur, please step forward."

A ripple of hushed whispers moved through the hall.

Lambert took Declan's place before their father, dropping to one knee and bowing his head.

King Erik lifted the scepter once more, touching Lambert on both shoulders, but this time he paused, inclining his own head. Beside him, Queen Penelope removed the soaring golden crown from her husband's head, carrying it gingerly to their eldest son. With steady hands, she placed it upon Lambert's brow.

"Lambert," King Erik said, his voice rich with emotion, "I anoint you ruler of Murdan, king of the realm, protector of the people. Do you accept this grave responsibility?"

My heart stuttered into an unfamiliar rhythm. Declan was not going to be king?

Lambert lifted his chin, his voice clear as he repeated the oath read out to him by his father. He accepted a kiss on the cheek from his mother, then stood as one of the attendants draped him with the gold and white robe that had belonged to his father before him. King Erik placed the royal scepter into Lambert's waiting hands.

Lambert turned to face the people of Murdan, standing before them now as their ruler. The king stepped back, lifting his arms in presentation.

"My people," he said, his voice ringing out across the hall, "I present to you, for the first time—King Lambert of Murdan."

The hall erupted. Cheers and applause thundered through the space. Confetti rained down from above, tossed into the air by the seated guests. Music swelled once again, the triumphant melody filling every corner of the grand hall.

I stood frozen, my mind reeling. I wanted to run to Declan, to ask what had changed, to ask if this meant we might have a future.

But he was busy with his family, surrounded by congratulations and celebration.

There would be a party that night, and I knew Declan would have responsibilities there.

But I hoped, somehow, that there would be a moment for just the two of us.

CHAPTER 37
DECK

DOWN ONE WOMBAT.

IT WAS AN HONOR—AND a relief—to be named Prince Regent. I was happy for Lambert. He had taken the place he'd been raised to occupy, and he was well fit for the position. In a way, I thought the commitment he'd shown to Celeste—to sacrifice his own reputation to protect her—signified his ability to put himself last. To do what needed to be done for others. And I had no doubt that Celeste would make an excellent queen.

More importantly, they were in love, just as my mother and father always had been. I thought that made a great difference in a monarchy, that those charged with responsibility for loving their people understood what love looked like in many forms, and nurtured it in their hearts and homes.

I looked for Lizzy after the ceremony, but the family was rushed out to our apartments in an abundance of caution since the mood of the people was exceedingly jubilant.

We'd have time to spend together and to prepare for the festivities that evening.

Dad and Mom looked especially happy, I thought. Part of it was certainly the news they'd received from Dad's doctors.

I still needed to update Lizzy on that development. After congratulating Lambert once again, I went to my room for a bit, eager to talk to the woman I loved. Things could finally be decided, and we could set forth our own plans for the future. I lifted my phone, confused when it began ringing before I could even unlock it.

Coach.

That was a bit of a surprise.

The Wombats had been winning. I'd followed the news online, and we'd even snuck away to watch a game on Lambert's massive television set, but I'd found it less fun than I'd thought it would be.

Honestly? I was jealous. I was supposed to be there. Those men flying across the ice, fighting for glory? Those were my brothers too. And I missed being with them, being a part of a team. I'd told my brother my head hurt and left before the game had even ended.

It was too hard to watch, too hard to realize that they really didn't need me.

"Hello?" I sat up straight, a reflex. I knew he couldn't see me, but I couldn't slouch while I was talking to Coach.

"Deck? How are you, son?"

He was still calling me "son." That was a good sign. "Good, thanks. Looks like the team's doing well."

The coach made a grumbling noise on the other end of

the line that sounded like agreement, but wasn't altogether happy. "Listen, you think you'll be back any time soon? I've been trying to give you time, let you work out all the… hell, I have no idea what the heck a prince needs to work out," he said. John had texted to let me know Joey had told him the truth and he'd shared it with the coach when he'd grumbled about my absence. "The thing is, Deck, we need you here. Or else I'm gonna have to go looking for a new winger, and I'll be honest, I don't feel like whipping some new guy into shape. I finally got you where I wanted you…" he trailed off.

"The team looks great," I told him. "You've been winning. Without me."

"By the skin of our teeth, Deck. We need a full bench. Look, I don't want to pressure you, but are you coming back or not?"

I didn't have a good answer. I hadn't sorted through all the details yet with my family or with Lizzy. If she wanted to stay here, with her mother, I wasn't going to leave her. "I want to." It was the only honest thing I could say. "Could you give me a little more time?"

There was more grumbling on the end of the line, and then the coach agreed. "Couple more weeks is the most we can spare. Can you keep me informed, please?"

"I will," I promised. "I'll let you know soon."

The coach hung up without saying goodbye, and I found myself smiling. I never thought I'd actually miss his gruff nature, but I knew it was just his way. And I did miss it. A lot.

I tried to sort through my thoughts then, and went to

speak to my parents. When we'd all agreed on a plan, I felt lighter. Now, I just needed to talk to Lizzy.

CHAPTER 38
LIZZY

NEVER SAY NO TO CHAMPAGNE.

I WAS NOT on duty that night, having already been assigned to the ceremony itself. I hadn't planned to go to the coronation ball at all.

But my mother, as always, intervened. "This is a once-in-a-lifetime opportunity, Lizzy," she said as she smoothed the fabric of her emerald-green gown. "Few people get to attend a coronation in their lifetime. And not only are you close to the royal family, but this might be your chance to finally speak to your prince."

"Mom, I think I should give up. Declan had plenty of chances to talk to me earlier, and I don't think we're on the same page about our future." I had begun to believe Declan planned to stay here, to serve his family in a royal capacity. Of course, he hadn't said as much, but then again, he hadn't said much of anything.

"I will never understand your reluctance to simply communicate," my mother said, throwing up her hands in exasperation. She turned away but then glanced back over her shoulder. "Wear the red lipstick."

Mom went ahead, leaving me to finish getting ready alone.

I had chosen a red sheath dress and a pair of very high silver heels. I wore what little jewelry I owned and put my hair up in the most elaborate updo I could manage—which, admittedly, was not very elaborate at all. I knew there would be women there wearing once-in-a-lifetime gowns, ecstatic to be part of such a momentous occasion.

As I walked myself to the ballroom, uncertainty settled deep in my stomach. There was something like dread inside me at the thought of seeing Declan happy with his family.

Didn't I want that for him? Had I even thought about him in the years since we had been children together, before I was sent to Virginia?

The truth was, I had. But I had never imagined I would grow as close to him as I had during my assignment. And I was ashamed that I hadn't been able to keep a professional distance. If I was hurt now, it was my own fault.

I stepped into the crowded ballroom, momentarily over-whelmed by the sheer abundance of the party. The festivi-ties were being held in the ornate palace ballroom, where more food had been gathered in one place than I had ever seen before. A five-tier cake—one that any bride would envy—stood proudly in the center of the room, a golden crown perched atop its iced layers. Buffet tables lined every wall, overflowing with decadent dishes, while the dance floor stretched wide beneath the glittering chandeliers.

At the very front of the room stood the royal table. A

throne had been placed for King Lambert, and Celeste and his family flanked him on either side—his parents looking proud, and Declan looking… gleeful.

The chandeliers bathed the room in warm golden light, illuminating glittering gowns, sleek tuxedos, and polished royal insignias. The scent of roasted meats, rich desserts, and champagne filled the air. Laughter rang out over the steady hum of conversation, and on the dance floor, couples swayed to the soft strains of the orchestra.

I had barely had a chance to take it all in when I felt a strong hand on my elbow. I turned and looked up to see Declan at my side, smiling down at me.

"There you are," he said.

"Here I am," I agreed, feeling ridiculously stupid, both at having nothing better to say, and for believing for so long that there was a path for us together.

Declan looked incredible in his ceremonial tux, the tailored fabric hugging his frame in a way that made my breath catch. He had always looked good in his hockey gear, but this was different. Regal. He belonged here, among the gold and grandeur.

I had never felt less like I belonged.

"Do you have a moment?" His expression was uncertain.

I looked into those deep blue eyes, at the full lips smiling through his beard, at the face I had come to love so much it hurt. "Of course I do."

Declan slid his hand down to mine, intertwining his fingers with my own.

"Champagne?" he asked, guiding me toward a bar.

I nodded, accepting the flute and sipping the bracing bubbles. I needed to steel myself. Being with Declan was always so overwhelming.

Declan gave my arm gentle tug, leading me through the room until we found a quiet table in the corner, somewhat shielded from the celebrations by one of the bars stationed along the walls.

The noise of the ballroom faded slightly, but my heart pounded in my chest. I looked deep into Declan's eyes and braced myself for whatever was to come.

CHAPTER 39

DECK

STEALING THUNDER.

I HAD MEANT to speak with Lizzy long before the coronation actually occurred. I needed to tell her everything —everything I felt, everything I wanted, everything I hoped might possibly come true between us. And yet, from the look on her face, I could see I had done a poor job of setting her expectations.

"There's so much I need to talk to you about," I told her.

"Declan, I understand," she said. And I saw it then. She thought I was ending this.

I shook my head. "No, Lizzy, I don't think you do."

"Tell me. Please, Declan. I've spent these last weeks so confused. I tried to tell you how I feel, but there's just never been the time. And then I thought, with your father, and with you being crowned..." Her eyes shone with unshed tears, and my heart clenched inside my chest. I had caused her so much pain.

"But I wasn't crowned," I reminded her. "I'm not king.

Nothing is different than it was before. And Dad—he's okay."

"He doesn't have lymphoma?"

"He does, but not the kind they suspected. He has a very slow-growing kind, and with management and treatment, his doctor told him something else would probably kill him first. That's what Lambert came to tell me the other day on the beach." I delivered this news almost gleefully, the atmosphere of the day infusing my words.

"Oh, well, that's… better."

"It is." I grinned. "I should have told you before, I'm sorry things have been so hectic. But now everything can go back to normal, Lizzy."

"Declan, no, it can't. Everything is different. Now you really are the heir." Her beautiful face was creased with concern.

"That might be true, but hopefully, Celeste and Lambert will produce their own heirs, and nobody will need me. I'll be just like Prince Harry, and you can be Meghan."

"I don't want to be Meghan."

I wasn't sure what she meant by that—Meghan Markle was amazing—but we could talk about that later. Right now, I needed her to understand. "I've been talking to the coach."

Lizzy's face did not take on the gleeful expression I had hoped for at this point in the conversation. But I realized that telling her I had spoken to the coach did not equate to me sharing all of my hopes and dreams with her.

"I've been talking to the coach, and my place on the team is still there."

"You're thinking of going back to Virginia?" Lizzy's eyes widened in surprise, but then her face fell again. "I guess that's great. If that's what you want."

I was royally messing this up.

"I do want to go back, but as you pointed out, I'm the heir."

Lizzy shook her head, and a tendril of dark hair escaped her elaborate updo, falling to frame her face. I lifted a hand and pushed it behind her ear. "I don't understand."

"I was hoping you might come with me."

Lizzy held my gaze for a long moment, and then one of those unshed tears actually spilled onto her cheek. "Declan, what would I even do in Virginia? It's not like I could take back my position as PR consultant for the team."

"Actually, John emailed and said that the calendar has been selling like crazy. Joey did a great job producing it, and the wombat is ridiculously popular. They've even made plushies of him now."

Lizzy smiled, but it didn't reach her eyes. I could see that I still hadn't said the right words. Part of me was scared to say them, but I knew what they were.

I took a deep breath. The woman in front of me was the bravest person I knew. If she could take down dictators in foreign lands, I could tell her how I felt.

"Lizzy, the thing is… I won't go without you. I can't. I love you. I've always loved you. You're the only woman I can imagine spending my life with, and I'll do it in Murdan, I'll do it in Virginia, I'll do it wherever you want to live."

I watched her face as I spoke. Her eyes widened, a small smile playing at her lips. But disbelief flared in her expression, and she still did not look convinced. "That's all I want," she whispered, but her voice broke, and she sounded sad.

"Then why can't you just say yes?"

I reached for her, but she didn't lean into me. Instead, she sat still as I rested a hand on her shoulder, stroking her collarbone with my thumb and hoping with everything inside me that she would fall into my arms and tell me forever was possible.

"Declan, I love you too. I probably have since I was a little girl, for whatever that's worth. But our lives are so different. We are worlds apart. You're… you're royalty."

"That has never mattered."

She shook her head. "That's easy to say—"

"That's because it's true," I interrupted. "My family might stand on tradition, and yes, I was born into royalty. I'm a prince, for whatever that's worth. But I will never be king. And my life will not be dictated by the regency into which I was born. I will live my life for me, and for you. And maybe that's selfish." I let my gaze drift to the head table, where my brother sat, Celeste at his side, the two of them laughing with their heads pressed together. "But I actually don't think it is."

"What will we do?" Lizzy asked.

Hope blossomed inside me. "Well, I'm going to need security if I go back to the states. Now that everyone knows who I really am."

"You want me to come as your security?" Lizzy's face fell.

I shook my head. "No, I want you to come to be with

me. But your background suggests you might be capable of managing my security detail."

We stared at each other for a long moment, and I still wasn't sure what she was going to say. Lizzy's lips trembled, her eyes filled with tears again, and my heart plummeted.

Was she going to turn me down?

If she did, I thought, I would just stay here. I'd give up hockey. I'd move back to Murdan. I would spend as long as it took to convince her. If that's what it took to be with Lizzy.

"I guess I do have the experience to do that," she said. I could see she was considering the idea.

I took both of her hands in mine and pulled them to my lips.

"So you'll do it? You'll come with me to Virginia?"

She stared at me, and then she nodded—the tiniest little motion, but the best thing I had ever seen.

"First, though," I said, figuring if I was in for a dime, I was in for a dollar. I stood abruptly, kicking my chair out from behind me and dropping to one knee. "There's one other thing I wanted to ask you. I didn't want to do it tonight because I didn't want to steal Lambert's thunder, but… no one's really looking, are they?"

Lizzy looked stunned, caught between laughing and crying, a huge smile spreading across her face even as tears poured down her cheeks. She glanced around. "Actually… a lot of people are watching."

It was true. Kicking my chair from beneath me might

have caused a bit of a commotion. We were definitely drawing a crowd.

I didn't care. Maybe I was stealing some of Lambert's thunder. But it was too late now.

I couldn't stop myself from asking the woman I loved if she would spend her life with me.

"Lizzy, I don't just want you to come to Virginia to manage my security detail. In fact, I don't really want that at all—that was just an excuse to get you there. What I really want, with all my heart, is for you to be my wife."

I stared at her expectantly.

Lizzy's face beamed with joy, but she said nothing.

I held my breath. One of the spectators stepped in close, leaning down to my shoulder. "Hey mate, don't mean to interrupt, but I think she might be waiting for you to ask an actual question."

The man stepped away again, and I realized he was right. I swallowed hard and tried again.

"Eliza Canfield, I've loved you as long as I've known what that word means. And it would make me the happiest man in the world if you would agree to be my wife." I took a deep breath. "Lizzy, will you marry me?"

She nodded first—just a tiny nod. Then finally, she said the words I had been dying to hear. "Yes, Declan. I will marry you."

I swept her into my arms, spinning her in a huge circle as the crowd around us erupted in applause and cheers.

Soon, my brother, my mother, and my father were at my side, congratulating both of us—though they had completely missed the actual proposal.

"Is this what I think it is?" My mother asked us when we'd stepped apart enough for anyone else to get a word in.

"I hope so," said another voice—Lizzy's mother. "I've been expecting this for years."

"Like, oh, twenty or so?" My mother agreed.

The two women laughed and hugged us, and then my brother and Celeste stepped in. "What do you think, bro, double wedding?" Lambert asked.

"No way," I told him. "Your wedding is going to be the biggest event Murdan has seen since… well, since today! Ours?" I looked at Lizzy. "We'll figure it out, but I don't think we plan to invite the entire country."

"Fair enough," Lambert said, clapping me on the back.

Celeste and Lizzy hugged and whispered a few words to one another, and then the music swelled again. The night was young, and the people of Murdan had a lot to celebrate. Soon, the dance floor was full and the spirit in the room was soaring.

I danced with my fiancée, letting the joy of the night fill me, giving me a feeling of completion I'd never known before.

Later, as Lizzy talked with her mother and mine, I moved to the bar for a refreshment. My father met me there.

"Son," he said, shaking my hand and squeezing my shoulder. "I cannot tell you how proud I am of you today. Of both my sons." My father looked happy, and more relaxed than I'd ever seen him.

"Are you relieved to be a regular guy now?" I joked. Dad would never be a regular guy, but it had to be a relief not to be king anymore.

He grinned at me. "A regular guy who's not dying anytime soon." A serious look flickered across his face, replaced a moment later by a contemplative look. "If nothing else, these last few weeks have made me realize how very precious life is. And more than that, how much those around us matter—family, friends..."

I felt the same way. I'd neglected my family these last years, but I vowed not to do it again. "I know I haven't been the most attentive son—"

"Do not interrupt your king," my father said. And then we both realized he was no longer king, and he amended his reprimand. "Or your father."

"Sorry," I laughed.

"I was about to say that I think the family you've found back in Virginia is every bit as important as the one you were born into here. And I want to be sure you know that you do not have to choose. You love hockey, and I know you love your team. If there is still a spot for you son, you should go back. If that's what you want, of course." His gaze drifted to where Lizzy stood with his wife, laughing. "You and Eliza."

"Thanks, Dad," I said, relief washing through me and making my elation over the events of the evening feel even more intoxicating. "I think that's what I'd like to do... but I'll come home in the summers."

"Perhaps your mother and I will come see a few games," he said, looking thoughtful. "Now that we are more free to travel."

"I'd love that, Dad."

CHAPTER 40

LIZZY

CAN I BORROW YOUR SOCKS?

THE NIGHT WAS BETTER than any I could remember or imagine. And to think—I hadn't even wanted to attend the coronation party!

Now, I was engaged to the man I'd loved my whole life, and our future was ours to choose. His title was official, of course, and should anything happen to Lambert before another heir was announced, Declan would take his place as King of Murdan. But barring incident, all it meant was a bit of increased security.

Strangely, I found myself eager to return to the United States. It wasn't that my life wasn't satisfying here in Murdan… except that my life as an adult had been mostly work. Okay, all work.

In Virginia, I'd had something close to friends for the first time I could remember. Joey and Clara and Drea. I'd felt included, if only for a brief moment, and it had been nice. Fun, even. It had been a glimpse into a life I thought maybe only existed on American television shows.

The King Father and Queen Mother (King Erik and Queen Penelope's new titles) had left the party relatively early in the night, and now things were winding down, citizens beginning to wander back to their own homes after a long night of palace revelry.

King Lambert and Celeste had bid us farewell, and as I returned from seeing my mother out, Declan caught my eye. There was a mischievous look in his deep blue gaze, and it sent a tingle dancing through me.

He approached, moving gracefully across the room toward me, and slid an arm around my waist as his nose lowered to nuzzle my neck just below my ear. "Have I told you how ridiculously hot you look tonight?"

I turned to brush his lips with mine, a deep sense of happiness filling me from the tips of my toes to the top of my head. Had I ever felt this completely satisfied? "And you, Prince Regent Declan, are devastating in that tux."

He grinned, raising an eyebrow. "Oh yeah? You like it?"

I laughed, wrapping my arms around his waist and pressing my cheek to his warm, strong chest. "You know I do."

"Well," he murmured, his voice a rumble only I could hear. "If you like, I can leave on select parts while I demonstrate how the Prince Regent worships every inch of his fiancée."

I leaned my head back to look at him as anticipation swirled in my stomach. "Which parts?"

His smile was sly. "The bow tie, of course. Maybe the cummerbund?"

I wrinkled my nose, picturing him in only the bow tie and cummerbund.

"Maybe the shiny shoes?" He suggested, lifting one for me to inspect.

"Let me see the socks," I said, and he tugged up a dark pant leg to reveal Wombats socks.

I stifled a laugh. "Are those Wilcox Wombats socks? The ones they sell at the games?"

He lifted a shoulder. "Maybe." Then he smiled down at me, his eyes filled with so much love it stole my breath for a moment. "If I leave these on, you have to keep your shoes on too. Have I mentioned how sexy they are?"

"Can I borrow some socks to wear with them?" I asked, poking him in the chest.

"Ow. You're ruining my fantasy."

"Let's go back to the apartment and we can make some new ones for you," I suggested.

He held me so closely I could feel his reaction to my suggestion against my hip. "I like that idea," he whispered. "It'll be my first time with a princess."

That got my attention, and I stiffened, staring up at him. "Wait, I'm not a princess."

"But you will be."

I hadn't even thought of it. That enormous gap between us was about to close entirely—and it had been as simple as Declan saying a few words. Maybe it had never really existed at all...

"Come on, Prince," I said, taking his hand and leading him toward the door.

"All you ever have to do is ask," he said, following willingly.

We walked the long halls of the palace complex, navigating together until he badged us through the family's private wing. We returned to the apartment we'd claimed as our own, and I kicked off the teetering silver shoes as soon as we were through the door.

"Wait a minute," Declan said, pointing at me. "I thought we had a deal about those."

I laughed as he made a face. "Fine then," he said. "I'm not going to wear mine, either. And you don't get to make love to me while I wear these." He peeled off the Wombats socks dramatically, throwing them onto the floor.

I was a little tipsy from the champagne and completely drunk on love as Declan pulled me into the bedroom.

"Would it be okay if I relieve you of this gown?" He asked, his fingers already attached to the clasp at my neck.

I nodded, smiling up at him. "And can I help you out of these?" I asked, my fingers working the button on his trousers.

"But don't touch the cummerbund," he said, and I erupted into another fit of giggles.

Declan unclasped and unzipped me, and then eased my gown from my body, holding my hand as I stepped out of it. He removed his jacket and tie, then pulled off his shirt.

"You cannot leave that on," I told him, pointing at the royal blue cummerbund around his waist, which looked entirely ridiculous, even wrapped around the most perfect example of masculinity I'd ever seen.

"Fine," he sighed, pretending to be disappointed as he

removed the cummerbund. Then he took my hand and pulled me into him, growling, "Come here, wife."

I didn't correct him. I liked the sound of it, and the word echoed in my mind as he spun me onto the mattress and laid himself over me, kissing me long and deep.

I was breathless when he pulled away, and soon found myself gasping as he worked his mouth down my body and teased around my core. My hands buried themselves in his thick dark hair as his mouth found its target and Declan sucked and teased until I could think of nothing but him. Inside me. Filling me.

"I need you," I moaned.

Declan stopped what he was doing immediately, and I was torn between telling him not to stop and demanding that he take me right this second.

I didn't need to say a word, because a moment later, he was sinking into me, inch by delicious inch, as his mouth teased the skin below my ear. My body arched into his, inviting him deeper and deeper until I felt his hips seat against mine.

"There," I whispered. "So. Perfect."

I could feel every centimeter of him, and the warmth of his body on mine added to the sensation as his mouth paused in its teasing progress to utter, "fucking perfect."

He moved slowly then, thrusting into me in a long, slow, languid rhythm that had me begging within minutes. When I thought I could take no more, he rolled, flipping us and smiling up at me.

I collapsed over his chest, which created an entirely new angle and set something off inside me. Pushing myself up, I braced against him while I began to move, undulating my hips to reproduce that incredible angle.

Declan was watching me, his eyes dreamy with lust, and his hands on my hips—not directing me, just moving in time. But when my rhythm sped up, then began to break down as every muscle within me flexed and shivered, he took over, thrusting up into me as he grunted out words I couldn't understand. And then, finally, as I flew from the mountaintop, he let out a roar and warmth filled my body just before I sagged into him, both of us breathing hard.

"How did I get so lucky?" he asked.

I was asking myself the same question.

CHAPTER 41
DECK

REBOOT.

LEAVING MURDAN WAS A SURREAL EXPERIENCE.

Never before had I left with such assured confidence in my path forward. And never had I left my home country with my future bride at my side.

Lizzy and I were escorted by a retinue of security guards, though my wife-to-be had decided she preferred not to play an official role in my protection going forward.

"Of course, that doesn't mean I won't be looking out for you," she reminded me when I asked—again—if she was sure she was comfortable letting others handle security.

"Of course not."

Lizzy wasn't entirely sure what she wanted to do in Virginia, but we both figured she had plenty of time to explore her options. Honestly? I didn't care if she worked at all. But given her determination and general skill at everything she attempted, I doubted she would be happy calling herself a housewife. Or a house fiancée. Or whatever one would call oneself when not employed outside the home and not yet married.

"This is all so unbelievable," Lizzy said as she held my hand, watching the crystal blue ocean drop beneath the wings of our jet.

"Which part?"

"All of it, Declan. Our engagement. The fact that you are going back to play for the Wombats. The fact that I'm coming with you?" Her smile was so wide and bright, I couldn't stop myself from leaning in for a kiss.

"I love you, wife," I told her, loving the way the word sounded coming out of my mouth.

"Future wife," she reminded me.

I raised an eyebrow. "That's nice too," I told her. "Not as definitive, though, you know."

I had an idea. A crazy idea. One I wasn't sure Lizzy would be excited about. But I leaned closer and whispered it in her ear. The smile that took over my fiancée's face told me everything I needed to know.

As soon as we were cruising, I stood and went to have a private word with the pilot. He wasn't on board with the idea at first, but I had some skills of royal persuasion that finally convinced him.

A few moments later, we were turning and then descending once again toward the Murdan airstrip.

My family was gathered around the table in the parlor, just beginning their midday meal. Celeste and Lambert sat side by side, and my mother and father sat across from them.

All eyes turned toward us as we burst through the doors.

"What did you forget that you can't possibly replace in America?" Lambert asked.

"Did you miss us so much already?" my mother added sweetly. She had already shed all the tears she was going to shed during our goodbyes. Now, it seemed she had switched to sarcasm.

"We did forget something," I told them. "And it's something we need right away. Something only Lambert can provide."

Lambert raised an eyebrow and looked between us, confused.

"Is it something I'm going to want to provide?" he asked, half a sandwich raised to his mouth, about to take a bite.

"I hope so," I told him. "Lizzy and I want to arrive in America as husband and wife."

The table fell silent.

My mother was the first to react. "Oh my goodness!" She jumped out of her seat and ran to hug us both.

"But I need to call MaryAnne," she said, rushing toward the phone.

"No need," Lizzy said, just as a knock sounded at the door. Lambert's guard moved to open it, revealing Lizzy's mother on the other side.

"I called her as we were landing," Lizzy admitted.

MaryAnne Canfield clasped her hands together under her chin, smiling at my mother. The two women embraced and danced in a little circle.

"I can't believe it's all happening right this very minute," my mother said.

"Are you sure you're not rushing things a bit?" my father asked.

Celeste stepped to Lizzy's side, wrapping an arm around her waist. "I think it's romantic," she said.

Her calm practicality seemed to put everyone at ease.

An hour later, we were gathered in the family garden, the sun beating down on our shoulders as Lizzy and I stood facing one another, with Lambert before us, ready to officiate.

Our parents and Celeste stood nearby, close enough to hear every word exchanged. The happiness inside me was effervescent. I feared it might bubble out of my mouth the moment I opened it to speak.

Lambert read from the traditional marriage vows of Murdan. "Do you, Declan Sinclair MacArthur, Prince Regent of Murdan, take Eliza Suzanne Canfield to be your wedded bride?"

I smiled at Lizzy, feeling the expression through my entire body. Nothing in the world would make me happier. I looked deep into her eyes, feeling our souls connect.

"I do."

"And do you, Eliza Suzanne Canfield, take Declan to be your wedded husband?"

Lizzy nodded her head, then added, "I do. Of course, I do. Yes. Definitely." She clapped a hand over her mouth as if trying to keep herself from agreeing even more enthusiastically.

"By the power vested in me as King of Murdan," Lambert said, "I now pronounce you husband and wife."

As I looked at my bride, a sense of calm, unlike anything I had ever felt, descended over me. When I took her in my arms and kissed her tenderly, it felt as if the world had finally begun turning at a rhythm and a speed that made sense.

We boarded the jet once again, a mere three hours after we had originally been scheduled to leave. We took our seats, and I held Lizzy's hand tightly in mine. As the plane took off, I leaned over and whispered, "I'm ready to go back. Now, I can properly call you wife."

There were many things to figure out once we landed—not the least of which was where we would live. Lizzy insisted, with my parents' agreement, that the safest place for us would be the eighth floor of the condo high-rise she had rented when she was last in Virginia. It was a little bizarre, considering none of the other floors had tenants.

"Don't you think it will be a bit lonely?" I asked her as

the driver pulled up to the building, where Arnold stood grinning, waiting to open the front doors for us.

"How much time do you actually spend with your neighbors, Declan?" she asked. It was a valid question. But I still didn't like the idea of being all alone on a floor in a tall building.

"If it really makes you uncomfortable," she teased, "we could just turn the whole building into one gigantic house."

"That would be a little excessive, don't you think?"

Lizzy grinned at me. "Like something royalty might do." She laughed.

In the end, the security team ended up inhabiting several of the unoccupied floors, and we agreed to lease out two of the ones below us.

We'd been home only a few days when I finally managed to finish everything I'd started on that fateful trip to Murdan.

Lizzy came home after running a few errands to find me waiting on the couch, two packages on the table before me, wrapped with gold ribbon. I also had soft music playing, champagne, and some ideas what we might do after she opened her packages.

"What's all this?" she asked, coming in and kissing me before taking a seat at my side.

I handed her a flute of champagne.

"A little overdue," I told her, taking the larger of the two boxes and dropping it gently on her lap.

"Ohh, I love presents," she said, taking a sip and then setting her glass on the table. "What is it?"

"I believe the purpose of the wrapping paper is to hide

that very thing," I said playfully. "If I wanted you to know, I wouldn't have wrapped it."

Lizzy whacked me with the back of her hand gently, and then began unwrapping the box. She pushed the paper aside and lifted the lid, and I couldn't help bouncing just a tiny bit on the couch in my anticipation.

"You got me a jersey?" she asked, wrinkling her nose at me. "I don't think they'll let me join the team, Declan."

"It's not your jersey," I explained. "It's mine. Turn it over."

She did. It had my name on the back over my number. "I think it's a bit small for you."

"Lizzy, I can't think of anything that would make me happier at the games than to see you wearing my jersey, cheering me on. And then everyone else there will know you belong to me."

"Possessive much?" She laughed at my fierce tone.

"Of you? Hell, yes. Which is why you need to open box number two now."

She dropped the jersey to her lap and picked up the smaller box, opening it so painfully slowly I almost snatched it from her hands to help. But this moment, I knew, would be worth the wait.

Lizzy gasped when she opened the little black box, revealing my grandmother's diamond engagement ring and matched wedding band inside. "Oh my gosh, these are beautiful."

"I know we're doing it a little backward," I said. "Mom gave them to me before we left the second time. I had them sized for you."

Tears stood in Lizzy's eyes, and I felt pretty close to crying with joy myself. "Will you put them on? Wear them?"

She nodded and eagerly removed the rings, slipping them onto her ring finger. "They fit perfectly," she said, her voice full of awe. "I love them so much," she said, looking up at me. "And I love you so much."

Lizzy climbed into my lap and proceeded to show me exactly how much while wearing my jersey and my ring and nothing else.

CHAPTER 42
LIZZY

WOMBATS ARE REALLY THE BEST.

MY LIFE HAD CHANGED SO DRAMATICALLY in such a short time that once we were back in Virginia, back into a bit of a rhythm, I felt a little whiplash.

"Whiplash?" Drea asked, frowning at me across the table at the Teakhouse Tavern, where I'd been invited to meet up with the WAGs for drinks.

(I'd had to ask, but I was informed that WAG meant Wife and Girlfriend and was told that if I hadn't been so busy all the time when I'd been here before, this would have happened much sooner.)

"Yes, you know, from everything shifting directions so fast," I explained.

Clara lifted her wine glass and grinned at me. "To whiplash, then. You sure look happy."

Joey joined in, and we all toasted as their smiles added to the warm feeling of belonging I'd been experiencing since coming back to Virginia.

"I am happy," I confessed. "Happier than I ever thought I could be, actually."

"I can't believe you're a princess," Joey said, bumping my shoulder. "I feel like it's wrong to just sit here drinking with you in a bar. Maybe we should be having tea sandwiches or something instead. Something fancier."

"Tea sandwiches?" Drea asked, wrinkling her nose at Joey.

"Like cucumber sandwiches. Or Vegemite or whatever."

"Vegemite is not fancy," Clara said. "It's vile."

"Agree to disagree," I said. "I actually really like it."

"You should try it, actually, Joey, now that you're such an Aussie-phile," I added.

"Am I? What is that? Is that a thing?" Joey looked ready to be offended.

"You do have a pet wombat," Clara pointed out.

"Wilma is not a pet," Joey said. "He is a member of the team who happens to live with us and occasionally disassembles our couch or poops in the laundry room." She tried to deliver this with a straight face but couldn't.

"What do you mean disassembles your couch?" I asked.

"He roots around in the cushions until they all fall off all over the floor, and then he burrows through them." Joey shook her head, smiling.

"I don't know how you can live with that thing," Drea said, rolling her eyes.

"You live with Rock Stevens," Clara pointed out.

"Point made," Drea laughed.

We talked for more than an hour, making plans to meet again soon for lunch and discussing Rock and Drea's upcoming wedding, which would take place at the end of the season.

"You're coming to the game tomorrow, right?" Joey asked me as we headed outside.

"Of course," I told her.

Declan had been so excited to get back to playing, he had been able to talk about nothing else for at least a week, and returned from practice each day acting like he'd been on a play date with friends.

"I'll pick you up on my way," Joey told me, her eyes glowing.

We hugged goodbye, and I drove home, back to my husband, still processing all the ways my life had changed for the better. And to think, it had all begun with a murder plot against the man I loved.

The world was weird.

The next night, Joey picked me up to head to the arena.

I was nervous, but I wasn't sure why.

"I know why," she said when I mentioned it, giving me a knowing smile from the driver's seat.

"Why?" I asked.

"Because this is your first game as Mrs. Declan MacArthur," she laughed. "And your first as a princess! The media's going to be all over you."

The news of our wedding—and of Declan's true identity —had been fairly widespread, with a few gossip magazines calling for exclusives, though neither Declan nor I thought that would be a good idea. Even without our participation, there'd been plenty of articles about the Wombat's royal winger, and one had even deemed him the most fascinating man in hockey.

I was just glad the man I loved was no longer the target of anti-monarchist rebels.

There had been a lot of debate about whether Declan's name on the team (and on his jersey) should remain Gillespie, since that was how the public knew him. In the end, it was my position that led him to demand they change it.

He didn't want me wearing "some other guy's jersey," he said, and no amount of rationalizing would make him see that if I wore a jersey with his number that said Gillespie, it would still be his.

"You'll wear your proper name," he had insisted when he presented me with my jersey.

The game was a hotly contested match with the Quill Boars, whom Declan informed me the Wombats hated more than any other team. "What even is a quill boar?" I'd asked Joey, but she wasn't sure.

"It's not a wombat, I can tell you that," she'd said.

We arrived at the arena, but instead of heading straight for the doors, Joey moved around to the back of her SUV. I paused, and when she pulled open the back door, I understood.

"Come on, Wilma," she called, picking up a small carrier. "You're on tonight." A snuffling sound came from within, and I saw the fuzzy brown body of the wombat inside.

"Oh my gosh," I breathed, bending down to peek inside.

"Hi, Wilma!" Wilma's little nose pressed against the mesh carrier, investigating me properly before he snuffled again.

"Does he stay with you until halftime?" I asked as we headed inside.

Joey nodded. "Once we're up in the WAGs suite, I'll put him on his leash. He's pretty well-behaved up there—usually." Together, Joey and I headed up to the suite where the WAGs generally gathered to watch the game. It was a much better view than where I'd sat previously, though part of me felt sad to be farther away from the action.

Wilma, for his part, was well-behaved. He waddled around, sniffing everything, climbing up on whatever he could reach, and making little snuffling noises that I found adorable. But soon, my attention was pulled to what was happening outside the glass. When the Wombats took the ice for warm-ups, my heart skipped a beat. Declan flew out onto the center of the ice, looking gleeful—like a child back on the playground for the first time in far too long. I couldn't see his smile, not with the beard and the helmet and all the gear, but I felt his happiness.

The energy inside the arena was electric, the tension thick enough to cut with a skate blade. At the end, the Wombats and the Quill Boars were tied with less than a minute left on the clock, and every single player on the ice was moving like their life depended on it. My heart pounded as I gripped the railing in the WAGs suite, eyes locked on Declan as he streaked across the ice.

He was so fast! The puck shot out from a scramble near the boards, and Declan took off, intercepting it at center ice.

The arena roared as he broke away, and ducked past two defenders, cutting toward the goal.

"Come on, come on," I whispered, barely aware of Joey and the others cheering beside me.

A Quill Boars defenseman closed in, trying to force Declan out, but he didn't take the bait. Instead, he faked left, his skates carving a sharp arc into the ice before he snapped the puck backward—right onto Rock Stevens's stick.

Rock blasted a shot at the net, but the goalie deflected it, and the puck rebounded—straight back to Declan. Without hesitation, he flicked his wrist, sending the puck over the goalie's shoulder and tucking it into the top corner of the net.

The goal horn blared and the crowd exploded.

My breath left me in a rush, my heart soaring as I watched Declan throw both arms into the air, his teammates mobbing him in celebration.

Joey grabbed my arm, shaking me. "That was incredible!"

I was laughing, cheering, and maybe screaming his name as he turned toward the stands, pumping his fist. It was too far to see it, but I knew he was looking at me. I pumped my arms in the air and screamed his name.

This was his home. This was where he belonged.

And as I clutched the jersey he'd insisted I wear, the one that bore his true name, I knew—it was where I belonged, too. Coming back to Virginia had been the right thing. For both of us.

At the end of the night, I waited. The team gathered for

the coach's comments, cleaned up, and met with the press before I was finally able to give Declan the hug and kiss I'd been dying to give him.

"Wife," he growled in my ear as he pulled me against his hard body.

"You were amazing," I told him. We were about to leave the arena, hand in hand, when a gruff voice called out from behind us.

"Lizzy?" I turned to find Coach Merritt waiting, a strange look on his face.

"Yes, Coach?" The coach looked uncomfortable, shifting his weight and rubbing a hand across the back of his neck like he was afraid to say what was on his mind.

"I just wanted to say that I'm sorry for doubting the importance of the PR work you were doing here."

"No, Coach, that was... It wasn't like I knew what I was doing." Coach had been filled in on everything—from Declan's true identity to the reason I had been here in the first place.

"I know that. But it doesn't mean you didn't do a good job. And I wonder, if you're gonna be around anyway, if you might consider taking an official PR position with the team." I looked between the coach and Declan, who was grinning.

I wondered if it would be a bad idea—too much proximity? But there was nothing I wanted more than to be near Declan and the found family I had made with the Wombats.

"I would like that—if you and Declan don't feel like it would be too much. Also, if you don't mind that I actually have no formal public relations training whatsoever."

"Well, I just figured that meant we could get you for a steal," Coach said with a smile. Given that I was now a princess and money was not my concern, he was probably right.

I looked at Declan, not wanting to accept without his input, but my heart was jumping inside me. "What do you think?" I asked him.

"That sounds great," Declan said. "But no pressure. If you want to do something else—something unrelated to the Wombats—I totally support it."

"Who in their right mind would turn down time with wombats?" I asked.

And as Declan and I left the arena, I knew it was true.

Wombats really were the best.

EPILOGUE: DECK
PRINCELY DOINGS

IT TURNED out that having a hockey-playing prince from a small island nation on your team equated to excellent PR fodder. Lizzy was swamped with requests for interviews, and Coach Merritt made sure I gave them happily. Most of the time, they were fun, light-hearted fluff pieces with Princess Eliza on my arm to give her perspective as well.

Relations between King Lambert and the United States had also begun to grow, and while there were no formal trade agreements or meaningful treaties signed, I was finding more and more people had heard of my home country, and for some reason that made it feel much closer than it had for years.

Add to that the visit Mom and Dad made toward the end of the Wombats' season, and the great schism in my life —and my identity—had all but disappeared.

"Son, this is a lovely building," my mother said as Lizzy and I welcomed my parents to our home. "Are you sure you can spare an entire floor for us though?"

"We can," Lizzy said with a smile. "Having a guest floor is a great benefit of the building, and since there aren't a lot of occupants, it's very quiet here."

"Unless there's stuff happening on the hockey floor," I pointed out. "But that's below you."

"There is a hockey floor?" Dad asked, looking confused.

I lifted a shoulder. Since being back, the building had evolved. We did have a few tenants, plus security, but that left a lot of floors vacant. Lizzy had converted one into a training gym where she and I worked out along with the security staff we employed. I also converted one into a man cave of sorts, but Lizzy and her friends seemed to spend as much time there as I did with mine. That floor was filled with pool tables, arcade sized video games, and lots of comfortable—non-squeaking—couches.

But the crowning glory was the hockey floor. We'd gutted the apartment, removed as many walls as possible, and replaced the flooring with a product called synthetic ice. Lizzy hadn't believed it was possible, but I'd actually created a room that would allow me to practice skating and shooting. It was here that I finally got my parents on skates for the first time. Of course, having been born and raised on Murdan, where ice rinks are not very practical given the weather, neither of them had ever stood on ice before.

"Son," Dad said, wobbling around the floor like a toddler on his first day at skate camp. "I have a whole new appreciation for what you do out there."

"This feels patently unsafe," my mother said, though she was taking to the skates much faster than Dad was.

Lizzy skated past them, turning to skate backwards in

front of my dad for a moment. "You're doing great, King Erik!"

"It's just Erik now, Lizzy," Mom reminded her.

Lizzy blushed. "You'll always be the king and queen to me," she said. "It's hard to break a habit like that."

The Wombats had a fantastic season, but didn't make it to the playoffs, so after our final game, we put together a gathering to crown the season. Mom and Dad were still in town, so they came along to Klaus Arndt's house this time. Mom and Dad were impressed with the house, and also with the matching celebrity-named dogs.

"Thank you so much for including us," Mom said to Coach Merritt as everyone lounged and hung out in the back yard under the heat lamps hanging from the overhang. Spring was just settling in, sending brightly colored blooms out to cover the trees and greening up lawns and beds that had gone dormant during the cold winter, but the evening still held a little chill and half the team was gathered in Arndt's kitchen around the massive marble island.

"It's a real pleasure to host royalty at a Wombats gathering," Coach said, looking between my parents.

"We host royalty at every practice, Coach," Rock reminded him, pointing at me. "And it's a real pain in the ass," he went on.

"Yeah," Sly Remington joined in. "The constant

demands for tea and crumpets, the never-ending waiting while he shines up his tiara…"

"Has he asked you to wait while he polishes his royal hockey stick yet?" Dad asked, clearly trying to join in. His question was met with stunned silence as the players around us tried to decide what exactly my father was referring to. Did former kings make dick jokes?

And then Mom burst out laughing. "Crude, Erik. Very crude."

The dam seemed to break then, and everyone let themselves laugh at Dad's inappropriate joke. "Sorry, I couldn't resist," he said with a grin. Dad had relaxed a lot since letting my brother take his place on the throne, and I loved seeing this side of him.

Wilma scuttled out from the side of the yard just then, and he headed straight for Coach. "This damn thing," Coach Merritt yelled, leaping onto a stool and pulling his legs up. "I swear, he has it out for me!"

Joey followed the wombat and picked him up, cuddling him to her chest. "Sorry about that, Coach. He loves you. You're his favorite."

"Great."

In reality, being a prince hadn't changed much about the way the team acted around me. John had pulled me aside when we'd gotten back though. "When you told me about your childhood, I had no idea this was what you meant," he laughed.

"Sorry," I said. "I wanted to tell you."

He just slapped me on the back and leaned into my shoulder with his own.

The celebration had almost ended when a familiar face appeared. A tall man with close-cropped dark hair and a beard that hugged his jawline stepped out onto the patio just as we were finishing our burgers. My heart dropped.

"Uncle Jericho?" I stood and moved to where he stood.

"Declan, my boy." He pushed his dark glasses to his forehead and grinned at me before enclosing me in a hug that reminded me of being a little kid again.

"It's so great to see you!" I'd invited him when I'd learned Mom and Dad would be in town, but hadn't gotten a response. Jericho had always been a little bit secretive.

Uncle Jericho greeted my parents, giving them formal handshakes and nods. I'd never really figured out quite what the relationship was there. I only knew Jericho was not actually related to me by blood.

But as I turned to Lizzy, ready to introduce her, it was as if the world suddenly clicked into a smoother orbit. Her eyes were trained on Jericho and her mouth had dropped open.

"Eliza," he said, smiling warmly at my wife.

I looked between them, and I almost wasn't surprised when Lizzy said, "Dad?"

It was a long night of talking, explaining, and reuniting after that. But Dad finally told me that the only reason he'd agreed to send me to the United States was because his top guard had agreed to take me and act as my chaperone for as long as it took. In the end, Jericho had retired in the states, never returning to Murdan. Or to his daughter.

Late that night, I held Lizzy in my arms, a strange

combination of emotion flowing through me. "I think I owe you an apology," I told her.

"For what, babe?"

"I took your dad." As I said the words, the guilt that had been growing inside me all night finally came out. "I feel like shit, Lizzy. I'm the reason you grew up without your dad?"

Lizzy, who had been lying quietly at my side, bolted up and flipped me on my back, straddling me on the Alaskan King. "Don't be ridiculous."

"But it's true, isn't it?"

Lizzy scowled at me. "No, it's not. Do you remember him from before? From when we were kids in Murdan?"

I thought back to all the times I'd hung out with Lizzy's mom… but I'd never seen Jericho. "No."

"That's because he was never there. He was always off serving some mission for the crown."

That was even worse. "So my whole family owes you an apology."

She huffed out a sigh, and repositioned herself on my chest, giving me a frustrated squint. "No, silly. He chose to be away."

"He did?"

"I had the same job he did, remember? I know how it works. They throw assignments your way, but you can say no."

"You can?"

"Of course," she said. "My mother and father never really got along. They did best when he wasn't around, and that was just what I was used to."

It didn't make a lot of sense. Jericho had been good to me. Kind, caring. "He almost acted like a father to me," I said, the guilt rushing back.

She shrugged. "I'm glad. It makes me happy that you both got that opportunity. To care about someone. To be cared for."

"But you—"

"I had my mom," she said. "And it makes me happy to think that my dad was busy taking good care of the man I loved for all those years."

I liked that idea. "You sure?"

"I'm sure," she said, finally relaxing back down into our bed.

"I love you, Eliza." The words felt so small compared to the enormous rush of feeling I had for the woman in my arms.

"A lot?" She asked, her voice coy.

"More than a lot."

"Enough for two people?"

I turned so I could look down into her face. "What's going on?"

"Declan, we're going to have a baby."

I hugged my wife tightly to me, happiness lighting the very air around us as her words settled into my heart. It was perfect. Everything in my life was perfect.

MORE DELANCEY

The Wilcox Wombats Series:

Book 1: The Wedding Winger

Ready for some ha ha with your hockey? The Wilcox Wombats bring the camaraderie and sense of found family you're looking for, along with snort-laughs and swoons. The first book features a star winger planning for his future, but caught up in the past. When his high school crush (the smart girl who always thought he was just a dumb jock) moves back next door, he knows he's in trouble. Grab it here!

The Kasper Ridge Series:

Free Prequel: Only a Summer

Book 1: Only a Fling

Read the Kasper Ridge Series to get your fill of small town steam with plenty of humor! Former fighter pilots share deep bonds and plenty of inside jokes. Step into their world as they join together to help renovate the Kasper Ridge Resort, a dilapidated mountain property in Colorado, left as an inheritance to Ghost, one of their own. But the inheritance also comes with a treasure hunt! Each book follows a different couple but each story builds another link in the hunt, so read them in order! Start with Only a Summer, which is free! Then pick up Only a Fling here.

The Singletree Series:

Book 1: Happily Ever His

What happens when the totally normal sister of a movie starlet meets her ultimate movie star crush, only to find out he is dating her famous sister? But it gets a bit more complicated than that. Tess's sister has brought movie hottie Ryan home for her grandmother's 90th birthday to show the world how quickly she could move on after her very public divorce. The relationship is just for show… but Tess doesn't know that at first. And Gran? Is a video gaming, weed smoking, take-no-prisoners firecracker who tells it like it is. Toss in a lovesick chicken, and you're on your way to understanding what kind of series Singletree promises to be. Plan to laugh. Pick up book 1 here!

The MR. MATCH Series:

Free Prequel: Scoring a Soulmate

Book 1: Scoring the Keeper's Sister

If you enjoy a side of sports with your sexy men, and want both wrapped up in a hilarious package, then you're going to love Mr. Match. Soccer star and genius Max Winchell has discovered the formula for love and built a dating app around it. Though he keeps his identity secret, he convinces all his teammates to try it… and one after another, they fall in love. First up? Fernando "the fire" Fuerte, who shares an enemies-to-lovers romance with PR rep Erica, who happens to be his teammates twin sister. Taboo, forced proximity, and tons of witty banter up the steam in this one! Get it here!

The KINGS GROVE Series:

Book 1: When We Let Go

Coming right up, a bit of Sequoia mountain steam mixed with small town swoon! Head to Kings Grove for quirky side characters, emotional love stories, happy ever afters, and a cast you'll want to make your neighbors. Book 1 features Maddie returning to her childhood home, only to be swept off her feet by a handsome and potentially dangerous stranger. These books are steamy and engaging, with a touch of humor. Read book 1 here!

THE GIRLFRIENDS OF GOTHAM Series:

Book 1: Men and Martinis

Head to to the dot-com heyday of NYC - the late 1990s! Join Natalie Pepper as she makes her way in the big city in this Carrie Bradshaw meets Bridesmaids coming of age story. Meet the girlfriends here!

The Digital Dating Series (with Marika Ray):

Book 1: Texting with the Enemy

Looking for sweet romance with a romcom kick? That's what you get when Delancey and Marika Ray team up! In this series starter, Elle is texting a guy she isn't sure she likes, but boy does he give good text. The only problem? She's actually texting her boss since "the guy" gave her his buddy's number instead of his own. Now she's falling slowly in love with the perfect guy and can't figure out why he doesn't seem perfect in person… Needless to say, hilarity ensues. Pick it up here!